THE CO'S KID

The City Kid

Clive Lewis

Dernier Publishing
London

Second edition
First published 2016

Published by Dernier Publishing
P.O. Box 793,
Orpington,
BR6 1FA,
England

www.dernierpublishing.com

ISBN: 978-1-912457-39-7

The City Kid

The Clay Kid

Contents

Contents

ONE

Escape from the Village

"Independence!"

The word itself seemed to have the magic of a spell conjuring up a brilliant future. John Ouma spoke the word aloud and the syllables sounded sweet in his ears. He wasn't thinking of his country's Independence Day, due to be celebrated later in the month; this was something far more personal.

"My independence," he whispered to himself, as he strolled down the narrow main street of his village, keeping to the shade of the acacia trees that edged the murram track. He began whistling softly between his teeth. Today was a day to savour: the day he had received the results of his A Level examinations – three good passes with an A grade in maths. It was what he needed to fulfil his ambitions.

He stopped at the local store where one could buy the basics of life – millet flour, maize, beans, fresh fruit such as oranges and mangoes, soap, washing powder and a few extras. The owner was dozing in a chair by the doorway.

"Eh, Mr Okot!" John called. "You have a customer."

1

The seated figure looked up, blinked in the bright sunlight and cleared his throat. "Who's that? Eh, it's young John Ouma. How are you, John?"

"I am fine, Mr Okot, and I am not so young: I was nineteen last month."

"But you are still a schoolboy."

"Not so. I have finished with school, finished for good. And today I am in a mood of celebration. I have passed my exams – with flying colours!"

"Congratulations, John. You know, you have become the pride of the village – doing so well at secondary school." He reached out to grasp John's hand and shook it vigorously. "So how are you going to celebrate?"

"Not yet decided. Meantime, I think I shall have one of your Impala beers."

The shopkeeper rose slowly to his feet and made his way to the large refrigerator at the back of the one-roomed shop. "The power has been off. You'll have to drink it warm," he called.

"OK, forget it. I'll come back when the power is on." Leaving the shop, John allowed his gaze to scan the familiar scene before him. The main street was a rutted, red earth road, flanked by a scatter of single-storey buildings, including one that sold mobile phone accessories. Even here, thought John, even in this run-down village of Mkandu, the modern world has managed to make an appearance.

Despite the presence of this shop, Mkandu presented, in John's mind, a depressing picture: progress and development had largely passed by this place. It was like being on another planet compared to the buzz and excitement of Kamobi, the

2

capital city. The village was in a time warp, stuck in the middle of the 20th century – or perhaps an earlier time when the British ruled the country, dependent on subsistence agriculture and lacking any prospects for young people with ambition. Even the road, with its trickle of traffic, led to nowhere important. The village seemed like a dusty dead end.

On the other side of the road, behind a screen of mvule trees, John could see the long classroom block of the local primary school and the uneven, grassless football pitch where he had so often played in the past. The school building was beginning to crumble and the corrugated iron roof was rusted with age. Close by was the local chief's compound, the only building in the area that had a tiled roof. Beyond that John could make out a small cluster of circular thatched huts, shimmering in the late afternoon heat. My home, thought John – my home for all nineteen years of my life.

It seemed amazing to John that he had spent so much of his life in that small compound, treading the same pathways, sheltering under the same mango tree, sleeping in the same cramped hut which he shared with his younger brothers. Going away to boarding school for his secondary education had given him a taste of independence, and now, with three good A-level passes under his belt, he felt ready for a complete break from the restrictions of village life.

John said goodbye to Mr Okot, and wandered across the road to the Mobile Phone shop, which sold lottery tickets as well as phone accessories. One side of the building had been painted in the vivid green and purple colours of Mob-Tel, one of the main telephone networks in the country, and the front had a banner stretched across the wall above a solitary window, announcing the company's slogan, "Join the Crowd. Join Mob-Tel." Next to the slogan was an image of smiling African faces, all young and lively, obviously enjoying life. Such an image seemed strangely out of place in this village, thought John, but even the older generation had learnt the value of mobile phones. Even his mother, who had never progressed beyond the third year at primary school and who spoke no English, loved her mobile phone.

Peering through the open door into a haze of cigarette smoke, John greeted the middle-aged man behind the counter. "Hi! How's business?"

The man snorted in response: "Business? In this place? It's like trying to revive a dead body! I'm leaving at the end of the month – let someone else waste his time here."

John smiled in sympathy. "You're not the only one leaving here."

"Who else is going?"

"Me of course! I'm heading for the bright city lights of Kamobi!"

"Good for you – although I wonder how you'll make a living there. Kamobi is bursting at the seams with people from the country trying to find work."

John couldn't stop himself grinning with delight. "I don't have to find it. I've got a job lined up. All I needed was some good A-level grades." He fished in his back pocket for a carefully folded document, which he waved briefly in front of the shopkeeper. "And this piece of paper, from the examinations board, is my passport to success!"

The man behind the counter rubbed his chin

thoughtfully and tried to sound pleased for John, but his tone hinted at a note of envy. "Good luck to you – but you young people have things easy compared to my days. When I was growing up. . ."

"Ah, yes," interrupted John cheekily, "but that was a long time ago."

"Not so long ago, young fellow."

"Anyway," replied John, "I need to top up my phone."

"How much?"

"Just 20. Can't afford any more at the moment." John paid and quickly left the shop, glad to escape its smoky atmosphere.

Once again John found himself scanning the all-too-familiar surroundings and reflecting on the possibilities that lay ahead. His early childhood had seemed a very contented period of his life, but education at a boarding secondary school, far from his home area, had changed his perspective. Living, for months a time, with young people from all over the country, many of whom did not speak his native language, had widened his horizons.

He had come to regard his village and its surroundings as backward and lacking a future. The ethic of personal ambition and achievement had gradually won over John's mind; he became determined to make a clean break from everything which might limit his freedom to lead a successful life. Even his parents, who had struggled to afford his school fees, were now seen as part of an old life that he had to leave behind. They had sweated most of their lives raising sufficient crops on their small area of land in order to feed their family and buy the necessities of life. John had no intention of joining them in that struggle, although he was grateful for their hard work, which had enabled him to study beyond primary school.

His attention was arrested by the sight of a minibus taxi bumping down the street and coming to a stop not far from where he was standing. Taxis usually bypassed the road through Mkandu village and people often had to walk from the main road two kilometres away. The passenger door slid back and three people got out, paying their fare to the conductor as they did so. One of the figures looked rather familiar to John, but he couldn't be sure until he had walked away from the vehicle. Then John recognised the young man and called out, "Zeke! Zeke Ochieng!"

A look of amazement crossed the other's face as he looked in the direction of the shout. Then he called out, "Is that John Ouma? It is – hey, John, what are you doing here?"

They shook hands warmly and grinned in mutual recognition. "For your information, Zeke," said John, finally responding to the other's question, "I happen to live in this village that time forgot. More to the point, what are you doing here?"

"I've got a widowed aunt who lives here – and I've been sent with some medicine for her. You know Mrs Alit?"

"Not well. She lives some way over there." John pointed vaguely along the road to where an overgrown track led to a disused stone quarry. "Have you got your exam results, Zeke?"

"Yes, and I got the grades I needed."

"Well done – and remind me, what are your plans?"

"I want to teach, John. So I'm off to Kamobi Teachers' College in a few weeks' time."

John looked at his friend with an expression of exaggerated sympathy. "Well, you know what they say about the teaching profession?"

"No — but you might as well tell me." Zeke was accustomed to John's witty or sarcastic remarks, because they had been at the same secondary school during their A-level studies.

"The saying goes: Those who can, do. But those who can't, teach."

"OK, John. Thanks for your support! So what about you? You got the grades you wanted?"

"I did — especially maths. Here's the evidence." Once again John fished in his pocket and brought out the now crumpled document.

Zeke glanced at it briefly, eyes widening at the high grades. He knew that John had not been the most hard-working of students but somehow he had the ability to focus when it mattered — in the run-up to exams. The document gave ample evidence of this. "Congrats on your results, John. So you're going to uni next year?"

"University? You must be joking, my friend. No. I am starting a job next month and will soon be earning a salary."

"What? Here in Mkandu?"

"Ha ha, very funny. Who on earth is going to give me a job in this place? Unless it's digging with a hoe! No, I'm off to Kamobi to work in the Ministry of Technology and Development."

7

John whistled in genuine admiration. "Wow! How did you manage that?"

"Well, I needed good grades in maths and science. I'll be working in the finance department – you know, accounts and that sort of thing."

"Getting high grades in your A-levels isn't usually enough to get a job straight from school." Zeke looked at John doubtfully.

"To tell the truth, Zeke," replied his friend after a long pause, during which he seemed to be deciding what to say, "a certain uncle of mine works in the Ministry of Technology and he..."

"...he pulled one or two strings for you?"

"You could say that."

Zeke was frowning. He knew such things commonly happened but he felt uncomfortable standing next to someone who was openly admitting to the practice.

John, however, seemed unembarrassed by his confession. After a few moments, he continued, "But, you should know, nobody is going to be pulling the strings of my life. My ambition is to aim for the top – and I believe it's up to me to get there."

"Well, you know what they say: there's a lovely view at the top but, if you fall off, you'll hit the bottom very hard!"

At this point, the two young men, who had been ambling aimlessly along the side of the road, reached the shade of a large mango tree. Here they paused and John turned to his schoolmate with a note of irritation. "Now, listen Zeke – or should I address you as Bishop Zeke? – you are slipping into your preaching style and I find that a bit annoying. All your efforts to make me join the Scripture Union group at school were a total waste of time, as you know well."

"That's true," Zeke replied, rather sadly.

"What you fail to understand is this: I don't want to be bossed by anybody in my life – whether it's God or a teacher or anyone else."

"But being a Christian isn't like being bossed around..."

"Zeke," said John, ignoring the other's words, "I have just had a brilliant idea!"

Zeke sighed; he could tell from his friend's tone that some sort of witty remark was coming. "OK, John, what is it?"

"I have decided to re-name this village. From now on it is to be called, not Mkandu, but Me-Can-Do. Get it? Me Can Do. In other words, if I set my mind to anything, I can do it."

Ezekiel Ochieng reflected on his friend's words; he knew there was some truth in them. John had always been a strong presence in the Sixth Form at Luboga Boys' College, and he seemed to have a method of getting his own way... especially with the girls at the neighbouring school. Even the teachers appeared to recognise his gift of leadership and, despite the rebellious streak in him, he had been appointed Deputy Head Boy, as well as the school's Entertainments Secretary.

Zeke hadn't been in John's closest circle of friends, although they had studied the same subjects at A-level and had shared many lively conversations on the subject of religion. John couldn't understand Zeke's devotion to his Christian faith, even when his friend had tried to explain the difference between religious observance and living faith. He also wondered if this "living faith" would last into adulthood. Even so, he respected Zeke's sincerity – he could see there was no pretence or hypocrisy in it. He also admired his friend's musical skills. Secretly, John was more than a little jealous of Zeke's guitar-playing.

At one corner of the football field was a large earth mound, long since abandoned by the termites that once occupied it. The top had been cut off to make a seat, conveniently situated beneath the rich shade of a flamboyant tree. The twitter of sunbirds could be heard among the red blossom of the tree. "Let's sit down over here," suggested Zeke. "Unless you're in a hurry?"

"Not me," replied John. "I am in a lazy, celebratory mood. Except for the fact that the power is off and I can't get myself a cold beer."

"Sorry to hear that," said Zeke, with a hint of sarcasm.

The two made their way to the seat and sat down. On the other side of the field, the primary classrooms were full of children in their blue uniforms. Teachers' voices were wafting across the field on the breeze.

"No more school, Zeke. No more being told what to do. No more being in a herd, like animals... you sure you want to be a teacher?"

His friend laughed. "You sure you want to be on that slippery slope of power and success?"

"I don't intend to slip down any slope. As for power and success... yeah, why not?"

"And what about your mum and dad? How do they feel about you disappearing into the big bad city?"

John smiled. "They are really happy for me! They were so proud when I got my results. You should have seen my mother – rushing round the compound, waving my results sheet above her head, shouting to the neighbours about her eldest son's marvellous deeds!"

"Mothers always seem to have the softest spot for their eldest sons. As for me, I'm the fifth out of six kids – so I don't get special treatment!"

"Too bad, Zeke. Anyway, I'm looking forward to getting my first pay packet and sending some money home each month. It'll feel good to be contributing a bit, even though I wouldn't want to live the rest of my life in this place."

At that moment Zeke's attention was distracted and he raised his right hand to cup his ear. A familiar song playing on the radio in a nearby homestead had been picked up by the breeze and blown to where the boys were sitting. "Can you hear that song, John?"

The sound of a rap beat came and went with the irregular movement of the air. The words could not be distinguished but both young men smiled in recognition. "That's Bobby K. You like that music, Zeke? I thought Christians didn't approve of rap or hip-hop."

"Depends on the words, John. I think that song is really good. Did you know I once sang it at the Scripture Union group?"

"No, I've never heard you play rap!" The rhythmic thump of the music continued to filter through to their ears. Finally, John asked, "OK, so what's so cool about the words of this song?"

"Shall I quote?"

"Yeah, go on if you must."

"Let's see if I can remember." Zeke paused and then, snapping his finger to create a regular beat, rapped out the lines from the song:

> You think that with your modern clothes and the way
>   you can dance,
> With your mini-skirted girlfriends – that life's a game
>   of chance.
> You think that popularity will get you anywhere,
> And when your pocket's full of money
> Then you'll never have a care!

John found himself tapping his feet and nodding his head to the rhythm. "Is that all there is?" he queried.

"No, there's another bit I can recall. It comes right at the end of the song."

> You think that fame and fortune will lead to paradise,
> But the more you get, the more you want – it
>   never satisfies.
> You can gain the whole wide world, my friend, and lose
>   your very soul;
> And when you die what do you get?
> A coffin and a small rectangular hole!

John was chuckling loudly. He wagged his index finger at Zeke like a teacher rebuking a pupil. "I see what you are doing, Bishop Ochieng! You are trying to sneak in a sermon without me noticing. But you see, I don't see why I should be ashamed of those things. Why shouldn't I improve my standard of living? Is it wrong to gain fame and a fortune? I don't think so. What do you think that song is saying, that earning a lot of money is a crime?"

"Of course not, John. I think the song is saying that money, fame, fortune, popularity – they're not necessarily bad, but all that stuff shouldn't come first."

"I agree with that, Zeke. I think girls should come first – but unfortunately you need money to get the girls, so they have to come second after the money!"

Zeke stood up, annoyed by his friend's dismissive attitude. "And what about the last lines of the rap? About gaining the whole world and losing your soul?"

John also stood up and looked Zeke full in the face. "You are free to get your satisfaction from prayer and the Bible and going to church – and even singing rap songs. But, for myself, I'll be finding my satisfaction elsewhere."

"And what about the coffin and the grave?"

"Well, Zeke, they are a long, long way off. Maybe, when I am on my last legs and about to pop off, I will do a bit of repenting – just to make sure it's not too hot on the other side."

"It's not like that, John. Getting right with God isn't a button that you can press when convenient." Zeke could sense that the conversation was not going anywhere; John's comments were becoming flippant. In any case, he knew that he had to visit his aunt with the medicine and get back to his home, 35 kilometres away, before the taxis stopped running on the main road, around ten o'clock at night. He needed to get a move on.

"I must go, John," said Zeke, indicating the bag he was holding. "It's been great seeing you again. We may meet in Kamobi one of these days."

"Probably not, Zeke. I don't suppose we'll be going to the same places in the city." John grinned mischievously. "Unless you're planning to visit the night clubs there. You could bring your Bible and preach to us sinners!"

"That's an interesting idea, John. I'll have to give it some thought."

The two young men shook hands and said their farewells. Zeke strode away towards his aunt's home, shaking his head and wondering if he would ever see John again. John turned back to the village store, having decided that warm beer was better than waiting indefinitely for the power to be restored to the village.

TWO

City Life

"J. A. OUMA" read the wedge-shaped nameplate on the desk. In the chair behind the desk, John sat deep in thought, his fingers rested lightly on the keyboard of his computer. The nameplate was placed at an angle on the desk top so that it faced the entrance door of the accounts department, as if it were trying to gain the attention of anyone entering the room. John glanced at his colleagues, Donald Tangu and Wilson Sembatya, both of whom seemed, like John, to have switched off from work. The clock on the facing wall was edging slowly towards five o'clock. The ceiling fan had stopped working and the heat of the late afternoon hung heavily in the room.

John stretched his arms wide, suppressing a yawn. He glanced at the open door on his left with its now faded nameplate: Senior Accounts Clerk: S. MOLO. Once again he found himself wondering how long he would have to wait before his own name was fixed to that door. More than two years' work at the Ministry of Technology and Development (or Min-tech as it was usually called), had not brought him the rapid promotion he had expected. The elderly Mr Molo seemed to be permanently stuck in his job, too old to be promoted and too young to be pensioned off.

The intray on John's desk was heaped with papers needing attention, mostly receipts and invoices that had to be recorded on the computer. The humidity of the late afternoon had reduced work in the office to a minimum. Since two o'clock John had dealt with four travel-claim forms, an invoice from a building contractor and little else – except to chat, on an internal phone, to a friend from another department for half an hour. His two fellow-clerks were also in go-slow mode.

John looked up at the office clock once again and announced, "Only fifteen more minutes of toil before we'll be free men again!"

Wilson nodded with approval. "T.G.I.F., my friend!"

"What?"

"You must know T.G.I.F., John. Thank God it's Friday! The weekend awaits us – with open arms." He chuckled mischievously, and the third accounts clerk, Don, joined in. All three young men had similar expectations of weekend pleasure in the company of the opposite sex.

Wilson had been folding a sheet of A4 paper in the shape of a dart, which he now launched across the room. It landed, as intended, on John's desk. John was about to screw it up and drop it in the waste paper basket, when Wilson called out, "Don't do that! You have to read it first."

John unfolded the paper dart and found, scrawled across the sheet, the words: "Cupid's Arrow – from your gorgous Rosepetal."

Irritated and somewhat embarrassed, John screwed the paper into a ball and hurled it back at Wilson, who continued chuckling. "And how is that girl of yours, John? Did I get her name wrong – is it Rosebud or Rosary rather than Rosepetal?"

"It's Rosemary, as you damn well know. And, by the way, you misspelt the word gorgeous. It's got an 'e' in it."

"Just like your girlfriend's name," Don Tangu declared, joining in the banter.

"As for you, Wilson, everyone knows that you are supposed to be the hottest lover in all Kamobi."

"I won't deny it," replied his colleague, still chuckling. "But, unlike you, I don't get stuck with the same girl for months on end. That is very dangerous. Before you know what has happened, she is presenting you with a baby and saying: *This is ours, darling, so now we must get married*."

John winced at the thought. Then Don chipped in with a further comment, "Or worse than that – you catch that dreadful disease."

"You mean HIV?"

Don laughed. "Yeah, HIV can be nasty. Very nasty. But I'm referring to something much worse. I mean the disease of falling head over heels in love. Then you begin to feel as though you cannot live without the girl. You are hooked, like a fish on a fisherman's line." He gave John a knowing look. "But then you will know all about that sort of sickness."

"Don't worry about me, guys. I'm not getting hooked. And marriage is not part of my plans – not with Rosemary, nor anyone else."

"Really?" said Wilson, rubbing his chin sceptically.

17

"Then I must have got it all wrong. You see, I had the idea from things you've said that you really cared for this Rosebud of yours."

John found himself struggling for the right words. "Yes, of course I do, but it's not like. . . that is, she. . ."

At this point the door to Mr Molo's room opened wide and the Senior Accounts Clerk bellowed at the three young men. "Haven't you three idlers got anything to do except discuss your romantic affairs? There are still ten minutes left before you finish work. I want those outstanding accounts dealt with before you leave the office today, whether it's five o'clock or midnight! Now get back to work."

The three junior clerks mumbled, "Yes, Mr Molo," in reply.

For a few minutes there was quiet in the room, except for the tapping on computer keyboards. Then from outside came the sound of squealing brakes and a metallic impact. John stood up in surprise and gazed down from the third-floor open window near his desk. He could see a bus that had stopped at an angle in the middle of the highway. In front of the bus lay a motorcycle and the motionless form of its rider.

"Can you see what's happened, John?" queried Don.

"Yeah, just another accident between a speeding bus and a motorcyclist. Guess who came off worse?"

"Is he all right?"

"What do you think? He's been hit by a bus, for goodness sake! He's not moving, anyway. Draw your own conclusions!"

The incident seemed too common to discuss any further.

Such accidents occurred every day on the overcrowded streets of the city. The three men continued with their work. John's thoughts, however, were on his girl and the time they would spend together during the weekend.

* * * * *

John had first met Rosemary Kimaga eight months earlier at the Kirikiri Nightclub. This had been one of John's favourite city spots since he first arrived in Kamobi two years before. If you had no partner, it was possible to find an unattached girl at the Kirikiri and to dance and chat until the early hours of the morning. The place was really special among the many clubs in the city: not like the smelly downtown nightclubs that served cheap booze and were attended by girls offering a one-night stand at a reasonable price. The Kirikiri was smart, respectable. Foreign visitors could often be seen there, and it was common to see white people dancing with their African partners. The girls there were always well dressed — even in the dim lighting you could appreciate the designer clothes they wore.

John's first meeting with Rose had followed a familiar pattern. "You have no partner with you? Would you like to dance? Join me in a drink?" At about 3 a.m. he had driven her back to the hostel where she stayed but, before parting, they had lingered over a long goodnight kiss. Then John asked her if she'd like to see a film the following evening. She paused, as if weighing up her reply. "That would be great," she said at last, and then smiled with delight.

19

The Sunday evening was spent in the back row of the cinema and not much attention was paid to the film, a fantasy about warring zombies. They agreed to meet the following weekend and so their relationship was established. John soon felt himself attached to Rosemary. He could not quite understand why he had these strong feelings for her and not the other girls that he had dated and, on occasions, stayed overnight with.

It was, he convinced himself, much more than sexual attraction. Rose was certainly attractive: she had a soft, fine-featured face, with a beautiful brown complexion. But John had known attractive girls before meeting Rose. So what was so special about her? He thought about her bubbly personality, her laughing eyes, her schoolgirl giggle which suffused her light brown skin with red. Maybe these characteristics had something to do with how he felt; he wasn't sure – but he knew that Rose had stirred feelings that he had not known before.

Within a short time she had become his regular and exclusive girl. Their friends regarded them as an "item", on the road (when they could afford it) to marriage or, at least, living together as a couple. John dismissed such ideas as premature. He was too young to think about settling down to married life, or even living together with Rose. But secretly he did wonder whether Rose might one day make a good partner for him.

In the meantime, John's priority was to get the maximum pleasure with the minimum responsibility, and, since he and Rose never mentioned the topic of marriage to each other, he felt secure from the dangers that his colleague

Don had warned him about. And Rose assured John that she took precautions to avoid any unwanted pregnancy. It was, thought John, an ideal arrangement.

It was nearly 5.15 pm when John finished his work and was able to switch off his desk computer. His two colleagues had already disappeared from the office and the place was quiet apart from the sound of Mr Molo talking impatiently on the telephone. John wished that his senior would not leave his office door ajar; it meant that Molo's voice was constantly heard in the background and, worse still, it meant that the senior clerk could hear what John and his colleagues were saying.

John hurried down the stairs, past the broken lift, and headed for the car park at the back of the office block. He was excessively proud of his red Toyota – not because it was a new model, far from it, but it was distinctive, with its yellow diagonal streak on the doors and its noisy, high performance engine.

Rose was already waiting for him outside the offices of a large insurance company, where she worked as a receptionist. The building was situated less than a kilometre from the Min-tech building, on the other side of Uhuru Square, and as soon as John drove up, she skipped across the pavement and slipped into the front passenger seat. He leaned across to kiss her but she drew back.

"You're late, John," she complained.

"I know. Blame it on Mr Molo."

"I blame it on young Ouma – sleeping on the job!"

John grinned and eased the car into the slow-moving traffic of the rush hour. "No chance of that, Rose. Do you know? Molo keeps his door slightly open all the time! Just so he can spy on us."

"You boys probably need to be spied upon."

"Anyway, Rose, what about tonight? A quiet evening at your place?"

"Oh, John!" Rose's tone was irritable. "You know I don't like spending a whole evening at that miserable place."

"Well? Where?" John was considering how little cash he had at that moment. His monthly payments to his uncle for the loan to buy his car were draining his resources, and he had little to spare. As for sending money home to help his mother and his younger siblings, that good intention had lapsed after his first few months in Kamobi. And he knew that weekends with Rose could be expensive.

"Let's go to the Kirikiri," Rose urged. "It's Friday, so there'll be a live band playing tonight. We mustn't miss them."

John sighed. There was always an increased price for live band nights at the Kirikiri. He thought about his slim bank balance, and the fact that he wouldn't get paid for another week.

"Couldn't we give the band a miss this time?"

Rose kept silent. But it was a meaningful silence, and when John glanced sideways he could see the deep frown on her face. He drove on in silence, neither of them wishing to speak. But John knew that this was a battle he was bound to lose. Finally, he said, "OK honey, I'll pick you up at 8.30. Are you happy now?"

She flashed a smile at him and planted a brief kiss on his cheek. "Thank you. I knew you'd make the right decision!"

The Kirikiri nightclub was a world of its own. Soft reddish light suffused the dance floor, where couples moved around in the half-light, sometimes to the wild rhythms of Afro-beat and sometimes to the sulky slowness of a sentimental ballad. The band, over-amplified by huge loudspeakers on the small stage, throbbed out its hypnotic beat, while spotlights hung from the ceiling would pick out the singer or instrumentalist in a pool of brilliant light. Tables and chairs encircled the oval-shaped dance area. In a long alcove near the entrance was the well-stocked bar; only here was the light bright enough for one to see clearly. The rest of the club remained in a permanent dusk of soft light.

John and Rose danced tightly, moving their feet in slow, small steps to a sentimental ballad. It was past midnight, and they had been dancing, off and on, for three hours. The dance floor was crowded, and the couple moved dreamily to the soft melody.

"I love this song," whispered John, releasing her right hand and putting his left arm round her waist.

"Didn't know you liked old songs from the 1960s," Rose replied.

"Is it that old? I didn't know ancient music could be so good. Anyway, it's really cool."

"You see, John – I told you the band would be good."

"Yeah – and pricey. Did you see what they charged for entry tonight?"

"Now don't spoil the evening by talking about money." Her eyes flashed a rebuke but she allowed John to join his two arms around her waist and to draw her closer.

The song came to its gentle conclusion and the stage

23

was entirely blacked out. A few seconds of complete silence elapsed. Then the singer announced from out of the darkness: "Now it's time I woke you guys up with some real music. OK, let's hit it!"

Four dazzling spotlights suddenly illuminated the band. The drummer began to lay down a thumping 4/4 rhythm, joined after several bars by guitars and saxophone. The singer grasped the microphone and made as if to swallow it whole. Instead he began to bellow into it, with delirious defiance:

Life is here to be enjoyed,
What are you worrying for?
Fun is not to be ignored,
Even if you break the law!

The movements on the dance floor swung into the pounding rhythms of the song, a fusion of rock and rap, and John began to gyrate with joyous freedom. He laughed aloud at his own wild steps and Rose shouted, above the roar of the music, "You are crazy, John Ouma!"

John could recall the first time he had heard the song. It was on his first visit to the Kirikiri two years before, when he found his normal self-assurance had deserted him, and he had hesitated at the entrance, nervous, wondering whether he should go in and investigate the club. And the words of the song booming out of the dance floor had been a sort of challenge which he could not resist:

Now you've got your freedom, boy,
To choose right or wrong.
Now the blood is hot in your veins

And life is strong.
Now your life is your own,
Don't hold back!
Just go on, just go on
JUST GO ON!

John loved to hear the song and to dance to its defiant beat. Its words of freedom seemed to grip his soul and he felt alive in a way that he never felt during the working week.

During the crescendo of the final line, the singer was crouching on the floor, face bathed in sweat, in a sort of ecstasy, both hands gripping the microphone as though he was trying to throttle it. The saxophone blared madly, while the drummer pounded his skins in near-frenzy. The song ended in a climax of wild, but still coherent sound.

The dancers clapped and cheered, as the group, faces shining with sweat, left the stage for a well-earned rest. After a few moments, soft background music and the buzz of conversation merged with the clink of bottles at the bar.

"John?"

"Yes?" John looked questioningly at Rose, who seemed reluctant to sit down.

"Is it OK if we go now?"

"What? Already?"

"I'm tired, John. And, anyway, if we're going to spend the night at the Nyanza Motel, we must book in before 1 a.m."

He looked at her in disbelief. "Nyanza Motel? Look, Rose, I never said tonight. I agreed to take you to the

Kirikiri – that's all. You know it's near the end of the month and I. . ."

"OK, John, if that's how you feel. Just drive me back to my hostel, then."

"I thought you were spending the night at my place, Rose."

"Well, you thought wrong. Can we go now?"

Rose's sharp tone stung John. He could feel his temper rising; he recognised the technique she often used to get her own way. In the middle of an enjoyable evening she would demand something extra – like a night in a hotel – and threaten to break up the evening if he did not agree to give her (that is, pay for) what she wanted.

When John first started dating Rose, he was very keen to impress her with his apparent wealth and high standard of living. So when they wished to spend a night together, he would readily book a room at a small hotel: not, of course, anything like a five-star establishment, but still expensive enough to make a dent in his income. He would book in under the name of Mr and Mrs Musoke: maybe they did look too young to be a married couple but the hotel owners never questioned them. Why should they, as long as the bill was paid before their customers left?

Rose never offered to pay her share, and John realised this was largely his own fault. In the early days he had always insisted on paying. It was a price he was willing to pay to secure her commitment to him. She was, after all, a very attractive young woman. Also he had exaggerated the level of his wages at Min-tech. Later on, when John was more sure of her loyalty, he would invite her to spend nights at his lodging, but she was never happy with these arrangements, for John's rented rooms were small and cramped, situated in a run-down area of the city. She would urge John to book in at the Nyanza or the Kifaru on Saturday nights. Having a girlfriend with high standards had its disadvantages, John quickly learned.

Once again, on this Friday night, John felt boxed in by Rose's either/or attitude: either the Nyanza Motel or an abrupt end to the evening. "Oh hell, Rose, you know I can't afford it until I get paid. How about next weekend?"

For answer, Rose stuck out her lower lip – a sign that she was in no mood to compromise. She just looked straight at John with her wide, searching eyes. And he knew, as so often in the past, that he could not win. He took out his wallet from his jacket and carefully counted the few remaining notes. He made a quick calculation, and after a few moments smiled.

"All right, Rose. Or should I call you Delilah?"

"I don't like the sound of that name. Wasn't she the woman in the Bible who cut off Samson's hair?"

"Yeah – but that wasn't the worst of it! Come on, let's go."

John was already forgetting his anger as he contemplated the pleasures of the night that lay ahead.

THREE

Promotion – with Strings

The following week was an eventful one for John.

On the Tuesday he drove his car into the back of a lorry and had to take it to a garage for repairs. When presented with the bill, he had a long argument with the mechanic about when he would pay. They finally agreed on pay day at the end of the week. John wondered how much he would have left to last him the coming month. For two months he had failed to give his uncle the regular payments for the purchase of the car and his uncle was not pleased. He had also borrowed money from two friends in the city in order to pay for running repairs on his car, and their patience, too, was rapidly coming to an end. He was becoming more and more concerned about his debts and his inability to pay them off. Life was becoming a struggle and he wondered how he might boost his income.

He thought about selling the car to pay off his debts – or, at least, some of them. But a car was a necessity for a young man in the city who wished to keep a beautiful and educated girlfriend, a girl like Rose Kimaga. John had lost count of the money he had spent on Rose – petrol for trips out of town, new dresses, visits to clubs and the cinema. But at least she sometimes returned the compliment and bought him things, such as his orange silk tie, blue designer shirt and smart tapered trousers. Of all his outgoings, John's expenditure on Rose and on their activities together was the one that he regarded as the most worthwhile and the most essential.

Two days after his motor accident, while John was thinking about his debts, he was summoned to the office of the Permanent Secretary of his Ministry. Hoping he hadn't done anything wrong, John ran up the stairs to the next floor and along the corridor to the big office. The man behind his huge mahogany desk smiled broadly and announced that John was to act as senior accounts clerk until Mr Molo's return from sick leave.

"Am I to use his office, sir?" enquired John.

The P.S. gave a knowing smile and replied, "Of course."

"Do you know when Mr Molo will be back from leave?" The other gave an evasive shrug: the conversation was at an end.

And so John found himself in the office of the senior accounts clerk at the Ministry of Technology, looking out through the open door on his two colleagues. They, understandably, were not pleased: especially Don who had worked at the Ministry much longer than John. They did not try to conceal their resentment.

"Good morning, *bwana mkubwa*," became Don's daily greeting, and Wilson would scurry to open the door to John's room, bowing his head in mock respect. "Bwana want coffee in his office at 10.30?"

"Cut it out, you guys," snapped John. "I'm only acting senior clerk, and when Molo gets back. . ."

"Molo gets back! He's probably kicked the bucket already, the nosey old fool," interrupted Don.

"But John is right," added Wilson, who was at his most sarcastic. "He is, after all, only *acting* senior clerk. I mean, nobody believes that he is *really* the senior accounts clerk."

John slammed the door angrily behind him. They could say what they liked, he thought. I'm not going to apologise for being promoted above them. And I'll make damn sure that, when the name "Molo" is removed from the door, my name is the one that replaces it.

He busied himself with the morning's emails and post, pretending to himself that he was not upset by his colleagues' hostile language. He wondered what they would say if – no, *when* – he was appointed permanently to the post of senior accounts clerk.

He imagined his name, in fresh gold letters, fixed to the door. He wondered whether Don could be right about Molo kicking the bucket. Was he so ill that he would never return? John knew it wasn't a kind thought, but he could not help thinking it would be a good thing. Promotion would mean a rise in salary, and that would bring him some relief from the debts that were mounting up.

The following day, Friday and pay day, John received a call on the internal office phone.

"Accounts Department, Ouma speaking." It felt good to have one's own office phone.

"Ah, Ouma," came a deep voice in John's ear. "This is the Permanent Secretary here."

"Good morning, sir," John replied in his most respectful tone of voice.

"Yes, good morning. I – er – I hope you are settling well into your new position of responsibility."

"Yes, thank you, although of course I am still getting used to..."

"Of course, of course. Naturally you will need time. However, I'd like to discuss an important matter with you. Can you come to my office?"

John's heartbeat surged. He hadn't made a blunder in his work already, had he?

"How... how soon, sir?"

"Now would be convenient."

"Right, sir. I'll be there straight away."

John's heart continued to pound as he made his way to the Permanent Secretary's office. With every step, he questioned himself. What had he done wrong, what error could he have made, since he had taken over as senior clerk? He could not focus his mind on anything which might have displeased his superiors – but what did that prove? By the time he reached the P.S.'s door his armpits were already sticky with sweat and the roof of his mouth felt strangely dry. He cleared his throat nervously and knocked on the door.

"Enter! Ah, Mr Ouma. Come right in. Here, please sit down." John eased himself nervously into a deep leather seat opposite the large, imposing figure of Yokana Mwive, Permanent Secretary in the Ministry of Technology and Development, who reached out his hand in greeting. John felt his own hand being swallowed up in the powerful grasp of the other's handshake. The P.S. was smiling but his deep-set eyes and protruding eyebrows gave him a rather sinister appearance. John felt intimidated in spite of the apparent friendliness of the man on the other side of the enormous mahogany desk. The broad smile suggested something lurking beneath the surface.

He continued to smile broadly at John, who fidgeted awkwardly in his seat and tried to smile back, all the time thinking: I don't trust that smile.

For a few seconds, nothing was said, and it seemed to John that the other man was probing his mind with his penetrating stare. Finally, the P.S. lowered his eyes and spoke. "Well, Mr Ouma – may I call you John?"

"Of course, sir."

"Thank you. Well, John, how are you enjoying your new post within the Ministry?"

"Very well... very m-much, sir," stuttered John, "although, as y-you know, it's only t-temporary." John stopped speaking, hoping that his words did not sound like a complaint.

Mr Mwive hummed throatily. "Hmmm... Mr Molo, I believe, is still on sick leave."

John wasn't sure if this was a statement or a question, so he made no comment. He was steeling himself for whatever the P.S. had to say to him.

Again there was a long pause. "I'm very satisfied with your work so far, John."

John's eyes widened and he tried not to convey any surprise in his reply. "Thank you, thank you, sir."

The other man had risen to his feet and was studying John with a deep, inscrutable gaze. The smile had not changed, however. "Yes, I am genuinely satisfied with your work. So satisfied, that I would like you to do something for me."

"Something?"

"Yes, some *thing*. You could call it. . . a special job. Very confidential, of course." The smile still remained in place.

John's heartbeats quickened in anticipation. But there was relief in his mind: the P.S. had not summoned him for the purpose of criticising his work. Even so, John could feel the sweat on the palms of his hands.

"It concerns finance, of course," continued the other man. "Estimates for the current financial year. Our Ministry is overspending, did you know?"

"No, sir," lied John.

"Don't be too tactful, young man, or I might have to change my opinion of you. To continue: we have a fund with the splendid title 'Miscellaneous Expenses'. You know the sort of thing?"

Yes, John knew − or he could guess: hotel bills for the "fat cats" on safari, new Benzes for top executives, extra houses in the country for junior ministers or their mistresses. All sorts of perks for those with influence. Perks that would never be specified in any document.

The P.S. did not seem to be embarrassed by John's lack of response. After a few seconds, he continued in the same, self-assured tone. "The fact is, John, the budget for those necessary Miscellaneous Expenses is all used up, and we are a long way from the start of a new financial year. So what can we do?"

"I'm not sure, sir." John could not risk suggesting anything.

"Now, you see, John, the Ministry of Finance will only give our Ministry more funds for official projects, and in such cases expenses must be carefully itemised. Of course, you know all this, mmm?" He hummed deep in his throat, smiling so intently that John felt menaced.

"Yes, I do know that."

The Permanent Secretary pulled out a drawer in his desk and revealed a thin A4-sized folder, which he handed to John. It was headed: *Oganu Bauxite Mine*. John looked at the folder quizzically. He knew very well that the project to establish a bauxite mine near Oganu, in the north of the country, had collapsed after the initial survey, six months ago. It had cost a large sum of money, and then the whole scheme had been dropped, after it had been shown that bauxite could not be economically mined in the area. "It's a rather thin folder, isn't it, mmm?" Mr Mwive hummed and smiled broadly. "I want you, Mr John Ouma, to make it thicker."

John dared not ask "How?" because he already understood and trembled in his heart.

"I would like you to add various documents from your department to make it thicker. You know the sort of thing. Claim forms for travel and car hire, expenses sheets, invoices, the sort of documents that you must be very familiar with." He pointed to the figure on the final page. "Basically, I want you to prove that *twice* that final sum was spent on the project before it was abandoned."

Everything was horribly clear to John now. No, he wasn't

being attacked for incompetence or inefficiency. Instead, he was being chosen by the Permanent Secretary as his accomplice in corrupt activity. Funds were to be diverted from the Ministry of Finance *apparently* to pay for expenses incurred in the Oganu Bauxite Mine project but *in fact* to pay for... to pay for what? Mr Mwive's private pleasures, no doubt!

John felt a lump in his throat and could not speak. The P.S. had edged round the side of his great desk and was now standing next to John, who was still seated.

He looked down at John and spoke in a gentle voice. "I'm sure you are capable of doing this little job for me?"

John found his voice but it came out like a squeaky hinge. "I c-can, sir, b-b-but...."

"But what, John, mmm?"

"Mr Molo, sir, he wouldn't approve of my using his files for this purpose. You know he's a stickler for correct procedures, and when he returns to his office, he..."

"Mr Molo," interrupted the P.S., "will not be coming back to his office. I have recommended early retirement for him, in view of his long period of service and his poor health of late. Of course, he will be able to draw a full pension. It is the least I could do for him."

John nodded thoughtfully. And he thought, how very kind of you, Mr Mwive. And how well you have got this planned out.

"Senior Accounts Clerk: J.A. Ouma – that will look good on the door, won't it?" continued the P.S., his smile widening.

It seemed that he had been reading John's thoughts. Here was the reward for co-operation: immediate promotion.

"Of course, John, there will also be an extra financial reward for you, as soon as you complete the documentation. It will help you to pay off some of your debts."

Amazed, John stared up into the other man's eyes. "How. . . how. . . ?"

"How do I know you're in debt, mmm?" Mr Mwive chuckled complacently to himself. "I keep my ears to the ground. It's my business to know such things. As I was saying, the promotion and extra money will improve your financial position. I'm sure that will be welcome to you." He circled back around the edge of his desk and sat down heavily in his deeply upholstered executive chair. He was no longer smiling, just looking directly into John's eyes. "Well, Mr Ouma, is it agreed?"

John felt in a daze. Was this really happening to him? It seemed that the P.S. had boxed him into a corner and he had no alternative. In any case, Mr Mwive's right hand was stretched out towards him in anticipation: how could he refuse?

"Yes, sir. Of course!"

Once again, John felt his hand being devoured by the powerful grasp of his superior.

After a few seconds, his hand was released and Mr Mwive sat back in his chair, smiling once again. "Good. Excellent. That's settled then. Here, take the folder and make a start when you can. Well, I think that's all for now." He stood up with an air of finality, indicating that the interview was over.

John rose to his feet and made his way unsteadily to the door.

"One thing more, John. This is strictly confidential. No one – absolutely no one must know about it – not even your girlfriend! Remember, just as I have the authority to promote you, so I have the power to. . . to do the opposite. I'm sure you understand me?"

"Yes, of course."

"Excellent. For now, goodbye, John."

"Goodbye, sir. And. . . and thank you."

Outside the Permanent Secretary's office, John paused to wipe the sweat from his brow. He looked nervously down the corridor to check whether anyone else could see him. No one was in sight. He breathed out heavily. It seemed that he was entering a new world of secrecy – a world where serious risk to his future was involved.

An image from a film he had seen as a young boy flashed into his memory. It was about a search for diamonds somewhere in South Africa. The hero – or was it the villain? – had been warned not to enter an abandoned diamond mine, because of the dangers of a collapse. The mine was like an open pit, shaped like an upturned cone, the walls terraced all the way down to its narrow bottom. Determined to find the riches he needed to lift himself out of poverty, the man ignored the warnings and climbed down into the bowels of the earth, where he hoped to find a rich seam of diamond-bearing rock. As he was chipping away at the rock face with his pickaxe, the upper layers of the vast well suddenly gave way, and the man was buried in a roaring avalanche of mud and rock. That terrifying image had stayed in John's memory. He couldn't remember anything else about the film — not even if the trapped miner had managed to escape.

John thought, I can still turn back. I can still knock on that door, enter that room again and say, "I'm sorry, sir, but I just can't do it. Please find someone else." Someone else to climb down into that pit of secrecy and corruption.

He raised his knuckles to the door, but, even as he did so, the icy voice of reason froze any further movement. *Are you a complete fool, Ouma? Do you think he'll let you stay in your position after what you've been told? You'll lose your job and then you'll lose Rose. Do you think you can get on in this life without getting your hands dirty?* The logic was relentless. John lowered his arm. No, he wasn't going to make a fool of himself. He wasn't going to throw away this one chance to get on top of his problems and to push ahead with his plans for the future.

He turned away from the Permanent Secretary's office and strode purposefully down the corridor to the stairs. He knew that he had to get started on this business as soon as possible.

* * * * *

John had a miserable weekend. So did Rose, who could not understand why his promotion to the post of senior accounts clerk should put him in such a bad mood. Of course, John told her nothing about the "job" he was doing in his spare time. But she guessed that something was weighing on his mind. He would not respond to her usual playfulness and seemed to find her company an irritation rather than a delight. Their Saturday evening together broke up at nine o'clock in a furious quarrel over something trivial. Rose had never before encountered the full force of John's anger. When he drove her back to her hostel, a stony silence was maintained. Rose got out of the car without offering a goodnight kiss and walked off without a backward glance.

As for John, he returned to his lodgings, sat down on his bed and stared vacantly in front of him, just as he had done the previous night. His thoughts were focused on the blue A4 folder in his leather briefcase.

He thought, "What the hell is happening to me? It's just a simple matter of diverting some funds!" After a long while lost in gloomy thought, he got up from his bed and examined his face in the mirror hanging on the opposite wall. Had he changed physically since his encounter with the Permanent Secretary? Certainly he looked more weary than usual; otherwise there was nothing to betray his inner turmoil. But inside he felt as though his reservoir of self-confidence was draining away, and once again the image of the miner being buried at the bottom of a diamond mine flashed on his mind.

John spoke aloud to himself. "I'm not going to get trapped. I just need to take all necessary precautions. I'm damned if I'm going to make a mess of this little job!" He opened the folder and began making notes. All the calculations would have to be transferred to computer but at least he could work out in advance what needed to be done. And, in spite of his inner fears, John knew that he had the skills and competence to do a good job for his boss.

John worked late at the office during the following week. As soon as his colleagues left, he would get out the blue folder from his briefcase and continue his secret work. And he found a certain satisfaction in the process of creating a fiction, of providing "evidence" that large sums of money had been spent in ways that came from his own imagination. The computer file on the Oganu Bauxite Project was steadily enlarged in parallel with the increasing thickness of the hard copy.

By the following Thursday John had more or less finished the work. He had created out of nothing proof that a huge extra sum of money had been spent on the project before it was abandoned. A claim to offset this sum would now be presented to the Ministry of Finance. Only an expert with specialist knowledge (and a very suspicious mind) would suspect that the evidence for the extra expenditure provided was false. Only Mr Molo himself would recognise that the signature at the bottom of various documents was a skilful forgery and not his own. And Mr Molo, of course, was gone from the Ministry for ever.

John leafed through the pages of the folder with a certain creative pleasure. "All my own work," he mused. "Not bad for a village boy!"

He felt relief as well as satisfaction: the job was finished at last. Soon perhaps he would be able to forget the whole business and let his conscience rest in peace.

He felt even greater relief when, the following morning, he put the folder into the expectant hands of Mr Mwive. The P.S.'s smile broadened and his eyes grew less shadowy as he looked through the papers which John had added.

"This looks very convincing, John," he said, finally looking up from the folder.

"Thank you, sir. I think you'll find the details are all. . . as they should be. And the computer folder has been thoroughly modified."

"Yes, I wanted to ask about that. You've put earlier dates on all the extra documents, mmm?"

"Yes — that was essential."

"Nothing to suggest that they were added *after* the project was abandoned?"

"Of course not — but I can't falsify *when* the files were added."

"Naturally. But then no one is likely to check up on such details, are they?"

John flinched at the suggestion. He wondered whether there was the hint of a threat in the P.S.'s tone of voice, but Mr Mwive seemed genuinely delighted with John's handiwork.

"A very nice piece of work, John. First class, in fact. I knew that you would not disappoint me. Now it only remains to extract the funds from the miserable tight-fisted idiots at the Ministry of Finance, ha ha!" He chuckled throatily. "But that is my business, not yours. Isn't that so, mmm?"

John smiled in agreement; he didn't want to go any further in this nasty business. The least said the better.

"You have earned a drink, Mr Ouma." Mr Mwive reached for a half-empty bottle of whiskey under his chair, placed it carefully on his desk next to two glasses. He poured a shot into each glass, and handed one to John. Then he opened a drawer and took out a padded brown envelope, which bulged with its contents. "Here is a little 'thank you' for your labours. I'm sure you will find a good use for what is inside."

John put down his glass and reached out his hand to take the envelope. He felt the pleasing bulge of a large wad of banknotes. He wondered how much it contained – how much of a "thank you" it would prove, but for now he dared neither ask nor tear open the envelope.

"Well, put it away, my boy. You can examine it in private. You don't want to display it to the whole world, I hope!" Again the P.S. chuckled deeply in his throat. "Now, let's have a toast, shall we? In the words of our vice-president on the topic of nation building: United we stand, divided we fall." He raised his glass, clinked it against John's and drained the fluid in one gulp, waiting for John to do the same.

John sipped his drink, more familiar with beer than spirits. He felt uncomfortable, distrusting the other man's apparent friendliness. He had a growing apprehension of what this big man with the big smile stood for – and of what he himself was becoming.

After a few minutes of aimless conversation, John was anxious to leave the room. He wanted to check his "pay packet". And Mr Mwive seemed keen to bring the meeting to an end, too.

John looked at his watch and said, "I had better be off now, sir. Will that be all?"

"All?" the P.S. echoed with a strange emphasis. "All? Well, I hope that won't be all! But yes, for now that is all. But for the future – who knows?"

John left the room with a sick feeling in his stomach — a feeling that much more would be required of him in the days ahead.

FOUR

Secrets and Lies

For a while, John was no longer in debt. The unofficial pay packet from the Permanent Secretary was more than he had expected, and he was able to resume his loan repayments to his uncle for his car. He managed to repay most of the money he owed to the two friends who had helped him to meet his garage bill. John began to believe that he would now get some control over his expenditure.

The nagging of his conscience began to fade. After all, it wasn't *his* idea to cheat the Ministry of Finance, and the sums that he had dealt with must be very small compared to the overall budget. Nobody was going to be hurt by his actions and, in any case, he guessed that corrupt use of government funds must be common practice in most government departments. Why should he behave any differently?

He recalled a proverb learnt at school: "The proof of the pudding is in the eating." Well, he had eaten some of the pudding and, judging by the relief it had brought him, it was proving quite tasty.

He and Rosemary had more or less forgotten their bitter quarrel, and John had made a point of buying her an expensive Ghanaian dress for her birthday. But their relationship had not fully recovered the carefree happiness of earlier days. From that time on there lingered a certain uneasiness between them – a vague suspicion that each was hiding something from the other. However, they buried any doubts about each other in dancing, drink and spending nights together, and the surface of their lives remained calm and contented.

Beneath the surface, there were disturbances. A month after John had completed his work on the Oganu Bauxite project, another high-ranking official in his Ministry approached him for a small favour – signing and stamping a claim form, which John knew to be false. It seemed a trivial matter compared to the Oganu business but it was still dishonest.

John was troubled by the request. "I thought the Oganu deal was a one-off. I didn't sign up to an ongoing process." He wanted to refuse to do it, but this seemed illogical when he had already obliged his Permanent Secretary. Besides, he needed a bit of extra cash for his planned visit to Kamobi casino.

Within two months he had done similar "favours" for three other officials, and in each case he had earned himself a useful tip; used banknotes in a plain brown envelope. He had not been familiar with any of these men previously. Each of them had approached him out of the blue but with a strange assurance that John Ouma would be willing to help them. He guessed that the Permanent Secretary had told his friends that Mr Ouma was extremely co-operative in financial matters.

Sitting in his revolving chair in his office, John occasionally recalled his predecessor, Mr Molo. He couldn't imagine the old chap getting involved in shady goings-on – he was far too straight, too honest. And Mr Mwive had presumably come to the same conclusion. So poor old Molo had to go! What a joke: losing your job because of being too honest!

If John felt any pity for Mr Molo it was the sort of pity one has for the weak and feeble. As the months passed, John felt increasingly glad that he had not bowed to his conscience; he had the courage to take risks to improve his situation. And he knew that he was good at what he did, both the everyday work as chief accounts clerk and his behind the scenes activity.

One day the Permanent Secretary summoned him to his office again. The large man was, as so often, smiling broadly.

"John, I'm happy to see you again. I hear you are something of a magician."

"Magician, sir? I don't do magic."

The P.S. chuckled deeply. "Ah but you do practise magic. Making things appear and disappear. And nobody can tell where these 'things' have gone or where they come from. Isn't that magic?"

John continued to look puzzled, but deep down he knew precisely what "magic" was being referred to. And he felt pleased by the compliment, because, without doubt, he knew how good he had become at covering up the frauds that he had facilitated.

"Well," continued Mr Mwive, having waited in vain for a response from John, "I would like you to practise a little more magic for me. I'm sure you can cast a few spells upon this little matter." At this point he handed John a wad of stapled sheets.

John looked at the title on the cover. He read aloud: "Proposed Diamond Extraction – Masinu Province. How long has this been planned?"

"Not long – so far the government has kept it under wraps. But the first stages are set for the end of this year."

"I see."

"Well, foreign mining companies will be involved and I think there will be opportunities to... er, benefit from their presence. Anyway, read the file at your leisure and let me know what might be securely done to... er, profit from this venture."

John's heart was suddenly racing. "I don't really understand, sir."

The other man fixed John with a fierce stare from his deep set eyes. "Oh I think you do understand very well, Mr Ouma. And I also think that you are the best man to deal with this matter. As I say, read the file at your leisure and come and speak to me about your ideas in a few days. I'm sure we can make this a beneficial process – for both of us, mmm?"

John nodded dumbly and left the room with a mumbled, "Thank you, Mr Mwive."

One thing was clear: there would be no escape from this pattern of "work" in the near future. And the truth, John was all too aware, was that he couldn't afford to give up this corrupt working even if he wanted to. He needed the extra cash. The increase in his salary following his promotion was not enough for him to sustain his present lifestyle, which had become more extravagant with the increase in funds. Sometimes John wished desperately that he could recapture the outlook that he had expressed in school debates, when he had bitterly condemned all forms of corruption and nepotism in the government. "Mr Chairman," he had argued, "there is no room for corrupt practices in this great country of ours. Let those who are stealing our future go to hell!" Not that he believed in hell – but it had sounded dramatic!

But now it seemed so different. He was a mere child when he had said those things, with no experience of the real world. As John made his way back to his office, he smiled sardonically at the memory of his old self. Ideals! he thought. They're a millstone round your neck. Doesn't matter whether they are religious, political or just moral, they are a drain of your freedom. And I intend to remain free.

John's enjoyment of his freedom grew stronger as the voice of his conscience grew fainter. The only drawback was the nagging fear that, in spite of all his precautions and skilful concealment, he might be exposed. The fear clung to him wherever he went. With every new corrupt action – and now especially with the Masinu Diamond Mine project – this fear chewed away at his ability to completely relax and enjoy life as he used to. And he couldn't put out of his memory the image from the film about the man who searched for diamonds and paid the price.

* * * * *

It was clear to Rose that John had changed. He had become more irritable and their conversations sometimes ended in silence, as though they had nothing more to say to each other. They had once actively planned to move in together in a new apartment block: now this idea was never raised.

One evening, during a meal at a Chinese restaurant, she decided to challenge John about his altered behaviour.

"John, what are you hiding from me?"

"I'm not hiding anything. What do you mean?"

Rose lowered her eyes, speaking softly, barely able to say the words. "Is it another girl?"

John stared at her in disbelief. The next moment anger overwhelmed him. "What are you talking about, Rose? Another girl! For goodness sake, do you think I could afford another girl when you have such expensive tastes?"

That made Rose angry. "Thank you for regarding me as a drain on your precious income!"

Other diners in the restaurant were turning their heads towards their table. John lowered his voice when he spoke next. "I didn't mean it like that! I meant — oh hell, I don't know what I meant. Look, there is no other girl. You're the only one I'm interested in."

"Apart from your work, that is."

"What are you getting at, Rose?"

"Your work — your stupid work. You work late so many nights in the office and can't see me because you have to complete some rubbish report! You seem to be living for your work. Sometimes it seems that I have to fit into your life when you're not too busy."

"It's not like that, Rose. It's just. . ."

"Just what? I don't like being second in line, even if it is work and not another girl who's the first."

"I'm sorry, Rose. But you don't know what sort of pressure I'm under."

"Pressure? Is that your excuse for your temper tantrums? Listen, John, I'm not concerned about your work pressures, but I am concerned about us. About where we are heading."

"What do you mean?"

"Nothing. Forget what I said. Let's enjoy the meal, if we can."

The conversation lapsed and the two continued to eat, neither with any relish.

In one corner of the restaurant, above the bar, a Nigerian soap opera had been showing on a TV screen. The sound was turned down low, and the few customers in the restaurant were paying no attention to it. The barman, noticing it was 10 p.m., pressed a button on the remote control and the programme changed to the local news broadcast.

"This is Channel One, Kamobi, and here is the 10 o'clock news on Friday 30th January." The barman adjusted the sound until it was loud enough to hear clearly.

John, who had been staring at his empty plate for a while, turned his face without any real interest towards the TV screen.

The newscaster continued, "The President has set up a special Corruption Commission to investigate allegations made in the National Assembly last week that there is widespread corruption in certain government ministries."

John felt as though a bolt of electricity had passed down his spine. He sat up straight, eyes bulging towards the screen. The news presenter seemed to be staring straight at him.

"The new commission will be led by Chief Justice Lukana Tagenza," the voice continued in a dry matter-of-fact tone. "It will have entirely free access to all government ministries except Defence, but it is understood that its focus will be on specific ministries, as yet unnamed."

John reached with a shaking hand for his nearly empty glass of beer, missed his aim and knocked the drink off the table. The glass shattered on the floor. John swore but continued to listen to the voice from the screen. "The maximum sentence for corruption and misappropriation of government funds was recently increased to 25 years in prison. It is thought that some high officials will come under investigation. And now for other news. . ."

Rose was looking at John's changed appearance: he seemed to be in shock about something. "What's wrong, John?"

"Nothing. Must be something in the food. I . . . I think we'd better go."

"What was that news report about?" Rose had not been listening, but it was clear that whatever had been said had disturbed John.

"I don't know," snapped John. "Some presidential announcement. You know I don't follow that stuff. Come

51

on, we're going." John was already on his feet, waving to a waiter to bring the bill for the meal.

John drove Rose to her place, without asking her to stay the night with him. He needed space. He needed time on his own – time to think.

As for Rose, she could tell that John's mood change had nothing to do with the food, but she could get no explanation from him, and, in the end, she was glad to say goodnight and leave him be.

Driving back to his rooms, John became conscious of his whole body being damp with perspiration. "My God," he kept saying under his breath – an expression of fear, not a prayer. "What did the man say? 'Entirely free access to all government ministries'? Free access!" And again he breathed, "My God!" But he knew of no God to turn to.

Back in his rooms, he paced the floor, talking aloud to himself. "I've got to think – think calmly. Mustn't panic. There's no need to fear the worst. Who knows? The Commission members may all be corrupt!"

John was an occasional smoker – but never in Rose's company, who couldn't bear the habit. Now he reached inside a drawer and drew out a half-empty packet of cigarettes. He lit up and inhaled deeply. But the smoke in his lungs had no effect on the fog of fear filling his heart at that moment.

"Twenty-five years in prison! To lose everything that's good in life! One might as well be dead," John decided. He had a good idea of what conditions were like in the country's prisons; he had once visited a relative who had been kept in jail for months before being brought to court on trumped-up charges. He didn't like what he saw: dirty, cramped, communal living, with no personal space.

John hoped he had done enough to cover his tracks — but what about his work on the Masinu Mine project? He hadn't finished; there were still too many loose ends. He knew his files could be vulnerable to a really close inspection.

He wanted to make a vow at that very moment — a vow that, if he escaped the notice of the Corruption Commission, he would never again enter into any corrupt dealing. But to whom would he make such a vow? The Permanent Secretary? Ha ha — that's a sick joke, he thought. To God? No, he wasn't such a hypocrite to invoke a God in whom he did not believe. If only he had someone to whom he could confide his problems and his fears. Maybe Rose would understand? He took out his mobile phone and called Rose's number.

"Hello, John? You OK now?"

"Yeah, I'm fine. Must have been the chow mein!" He attempted a laugh but it sounded forced. "Rose, I just..."

"Yes?"

"I just wanted to... you know, to say sorry for ending the evening like that."

"Is that all?"

John paused. He knew, with sudden total clarity, that he dared not confide in her. "Yeah, that's all, Rose. I'll call you tomorrow."

"OK, John. Goodnight."

"Goodnight, Rose."

The following day, a Saturday, John spent the morning and most of the afternoon in his office, checking and rechecking his computer files. He had to do everything he could to keep himself secure from arrest and imprisonment. Everything *seemed* in good order, but he had no idea how expert or how thorough members of the Corruption Commission would prove to be in their investigations. However, he felt somewhat reassured by the time he left the office. The panic had gone and the fear had been replaced by a vague awareness that the future was uncertain.

Finally he remembered to phone Rose at four o'clock. He was disappointed to find that she had arranged to go out with a few friends from her workplace, but she agreed to meet up at the bar of the Kilima Hotel on Sunday afternoon.

By then John's self-confidence had returned and their conversation was both lively and relaxed. However, his main concern was his present lack of funds. In spite of his increased income, official or unofficial, John was spending beyond his means again and he was in serious debt. He knew he had to disappoint Rose and he wondered how she would take it. Finally, John chose the moment.

"Rose," he said, after taking a deep breath.

"Yes, John?"

"You remember I promised to take you to the Mbuluwo game park next weekend?"

"Oh yes. I'd forgotten about that."

John suppressed his surprise at her forgetting such a trip. "Well," he continued, "I'm afraid we'll have to postpone it. My salary is all spent for this month. Honestly, I'm just about broke."

"I see." Her tone did not express the disappointment or resentment that John was anticipating. He had expected an

54

outburst about broken promises, about his "stupid work" at the office.

"You don't mind too much, Rose?"

Rose was looking down into her glass, so that John could not see her eyes. She seemed to be searching for the right words to say. "Well, John, in a way I do, but you can't spend money if you haven't got it, can you?"

"You aren't usually so logical as that, when it comes to spending my money!"

"Stop being nasty," snapped Rose, finally looking at John directly. "I'm just trying to be helpful." John kept quiet, but he was thinking, When were you ever helpful in money matters?

Rose continued, "I don't want to be a constant burden to you, John, and anyway. . ."

"Anyway what?" John's eyes widened at the oddness of her tone.

"What I mean is, it's your life."

"My life?" echoed John. "What is that supposed to mean? It's our life that we are talking about." John was disturbed now; he could not focus his mind on what the girl was implying. He leaned across the table and took hold of Rose's hand, which he gripped far too tightly.

Rose snatched her hand out of his grasp. "Let go of me!" she snapped. "I'm not your property!"

He sat back in his chair and stared at her in confusion, his right hand limp upon his thigh. He had hoped that Rose's company would bring some relief from the worry that he had been wrestling with. Instead, it was bringing more worry, more confusion. They were behaving like strangers, not lovers. They were drawing each other into one of their pointless quarrels.

"What are you so upset about, Rose?" he asked at last. "Have I ever treated you as 'my property'?"

Rose was staring again into her empty glass, as though it might contain an answer. Then she looked up at John and gave him one of her brilliant, disarming smiles. "Of course not, darling. I was just being silly."

Once again she was being sweet and engaging, and her eyes seemed to speak words of love.

She pushed her glass across the table. "How about buying me another drink?"

While John was at the bar, she was being closely watched by a handsome middle-aged man in an expensive suit, seated alone at another table. She turned in his direction and acknowledged his presence with a discreet nod of the head. He raised his right hand ever so slightly and smiled.

FIVE

Overthrown

"So you've been overthrown at last!" said Wilson Sembatya to John, as he was about to enter his office.

John looked sharply at his junior colleague, who was grinning mischievously. "What's that you say?"

"I said you've been overthrown."

For a fleeting moment John feared that Wilson was referring to his job. But his colleague's next words made it clear that his comment had nothing to do with his job. "Don't say that I didn't warn you, Mr Senior Accounts Clerk. Girls are all the same. They squeeze you dry of all your money, if you let them, and then, when you're dry, they. . . er. . . look for other well-watered sources."

"Keep your stupid riddles to yourself, Wilson," muttered John, pretending to be indifferent. He was about to close his office door behind him when Wilson called out loudly.

"Here's one more riddle for you, before you hide yourself in your little room."

John paused, the door still ajar, and looked through the

gap at Wilson's grinning face. "What?"

"If you try to pick a rose – a ROSE I say – then don't be surprised if you get pricked by HER thorns. Isn't that correct, John?"

John, furious, strode back in the direction of his colleague's desk and bellowed into his face. "Damn you, Wilson Sembatya, if you've got something to say, just say it in plain language!"

"All right, Mr Big," replied Wilson, whose grin had become a mocking sneer and who showed no concern at John's threatening stance. "Here it is in plain, simple English, which even you should be able to understand. Your ever-faithful, beautiful and most desirable girlfriend, Miss Rose Kimaga, has got herself another guy, with more money and more influence than you'll ever have. So I repeat: you have been overthrown."

Wilson quickly retreated behind his chair as John made a lunge for him across the desk. "You liar. I'm going to fix you, Sembatya!"

"Before you try to fix me," continued Wilson, who now felt safe behind his office chair, "may I suggest that you ask your Rose where she was on Saturday afternoon when you were so busy with all your extra work in your office? Or may I suggest that you watch the movements of a certain junior minister from the Ministry of Trade and Commerce?"

"Who – who do you mean?"

"Surely you have heard of the Right Honourable Yakobo Njoru? He is well known in the city for his excellent taste in the opposite sex. He's not young, I admit, but extremely rich. Well, he has added your fragrant Rose to his conquests.

You still don't believe me? Why don't you ask Rose herself? And then, if you find I have invented this whole story, I will give you permission to 'fix' me!"

John's hands were trembling. He felt sick with impotent rage, because he knew he couldn't assault a colleague – at least, not at work. And his hate for Wilson was tempered by a nagging fear that he might be telling the truth.

For several seconds John remained rooted to the spot, quivering with doubt and fury. Then the telephone rang in his office.

"Your phone," remarked Don.

John turned away and returned to his office, slamming the door behind him.

* * * * *

After work, John waited in vain for Rose to arrive at their usual meeting place. He rang her number and was surprised to hear the message: *I'm sorry. This number is not currently available. Please try later.*

He drove to her lodgings, a fuzz of uncertainty clouding his thoughts. He rushed up the stairs to her room and knocked on the door. There was no reply. He knocked more loudly, then banged with his fist. "Rose! Rose! It's John! Are you there?"

The noise had disturbed the girl living in the adjacent room and she looked out to see who was calling out so loudly.

"Oh, hello Christina. Any idea where Rose might be?"

Rose's neighbour stood speechless for a while. Then she stammered, "I – I th-thought th-that she was with you."

"With me? Yes, we were supposed to meet after work!"

"No, I mean, I thought that — you were together."

John was losing his cool, and his tone became more impatient. "What do you mean? Of course, we're together."

"No, John, I mean I thought that she had moved in with you — at your place."

"Why on earth would you think that?" Once again there was an embarrassed silence. "Just tell me, Christina, what are you getting at?"

"Well, she moved out last night, with most of her things. She took a taxi — at least I thought it was a taxi, a big Mercedes. I thought she was going to your place." She looked at John's wild expression, and then added softly, "I'm sorry."

John did not reply. He turned on his heels and dashed down the stairs. He got back in his car and drove like a man possessed to his lodgings, hoping against hope that Rose would be there, waiting for him. She had a key so she could easily let herself in.

But Rose was not there. Nor could he find her at the Kirikiri club, nor the Kilima Hotel, nor the Cantonese Restaurant, nor any of the places where they liked to unwind. He had a fearful vision of her being in a road accident, but then he recalled what Christina had said: she took *most of her things*. So where was she going to stay? And what about those sneering comments of Wilson about a junior minister named Yakobo Njoru?

Late that evening, while John was sitting on his bed in an emotional agony of doubt, he decided to phone one or two friends, to find out if they knew anything about Rose.

He had left his phone in his car, so he made his way to the side street where he usually parked it. He found a message on his phone from Rose: *Hi, John. I just wanted to say: thanks for all the fun we've had together. It's been great, but all good things have to end sometime. I'm sure you'll find someone else soon. Please don't try to contact me. Love and kisses. Goodbye.*

John sat in the driving seat of his car and rested his head on the steering wheel. He kept repeating, under his breath, "Love and kisses! Love and kisses!" And he thought, "What sort of love is that?" He began banging the palms of his hands on the dashboard, and felt the anger bubbling up inside him, overwhelming his initial shock.

"She can't do this to me! Who does she think she is? Rose! Rose! I say you can't do this to me! You'll regret this. You won't get away with this!"

When the spasm of rage had passed, John felt utterly drained. He sat motionless, staring through the windscreen at the dark outline of the car parked in front of his.

Later he found himself back in his rooms. He couldn't recall when he had returned and had no idea how long he had sat, in a daze, in his car. It was already past ten o'clock. His phone was still gripped in his right hand, so he found Rose's number and pressed the green button. A lingering hope that perhaps Rose might answer was quickly snuffed out by the message: *This number has not been recognised. Please check that you have dialled correctly.*

John lay on his bed, physically weary, while his brain buzzed with unanswered questions. He tried to recall whether Rose had given indications of planning a break-up.

He raged at the thought that his colleagues at work somehow knew about what was going on, while he had remained in ignorance. "The know-all bastards! And I shall have to face them in the morning!"

He slept fitfully, fully clothed, and throughout the night his thoughts and dreams were tormented by images of loss and humiliation. But still he clung to a vague hope that Rose would quickly realise her mistake and return to him. He imagined her on her knees, weeping with regret, reaching out longingly towards him. And then the vision was shattered by the leering face of Wilson Sembatya declaring, "If you pick a rose, don't be surprised to get pricked by her thorns."

The following morning he managed to get to his office before his colleagues arrived. He shut his office door and tried to bury himself in his work. He couldn't concentrate properly. His mind was darting in all directions like a headless chicken. Even his concern over the Corruption Commission had been pushed into the background, as he struggled to come to terms with the thought that Rose had dumped him. "Come to terms? Why, why should I just accept the situation? Wait, there's something I can do!"

He surfed through various internet sites on his computer and soon found what he was looking for. "Ah, here we are: 'The Right Honourable Yakobo Njoru, Deputy Minister at the Ministry of Trade and Commerce. Home address: 230 Panorama Road, Kamobi.' So that's where that creature lives."

Panorama Road ran through one of the most exclusive areas of Kamobi, high on a hill overlooking the centre of the city. It offered spectacular views – and also spectacular prices for anyone wishing to buy a house there. John determined to gather proof of what his colleagues had asserted before he believed their story. And maybe there was a chance he could see Rose and sort everything out.

John had no precise plan of what to do but, immediately after work, he drove out of the city centre towards the hill where the Right Honourable Njoru – and *perhaps* Rose Kimaga – lived. Most of the houses lining the street were mansions – huge, impressive buildings with extensive grounds and high walls and iron gates guarded by men with rifles. He left his car in a side-turning and walked further up the hill, glancing furtively at the entrances that he passed. Finally he found number 230: not as impressive as some of the dwellings but grand enough. In front of the gate was a wide grass verge and pavement with a clump of mvule trees offering some cover. Here John waited, pretending to read a newspaper. Every so often he peered between the trunks of the trees to see if anyone was entering or emerging from the house. The watchman was dozing in his sentry box to one side of the high gate. Razor wire ran along the length of the exterior wall.

For more than an hour John waited with increasing frustration. He wondered whether he could find the nerve to approach the watchman and ask to see Miss Kimaga. Then, as dusk was beginning to thicken, a cream-coloured Mercedes drove up to the gate. The driver sounded his horn and the watchman rushed to open the gate.

That's him – that's Njoru, thought John, peering at the man seated behind the driver.

The car disappeared into the compound and the gate

was closed once more. John was tortured with uncertainty: *What do I do now?*

He had no plan of action. He began to realise the folly of coming to this house. And yet he was reluctant to return to his place without finding out for certain whether Rose was living here or not. After ten minutes of agonising uncertainty, John finally decided that he would approach the watchman and ask if a lady named Rose was living there. Just as he was emerging from his hiding place, the gates were opened again, and the cream-coloured Mercedes drove out of the compound. John ducked behind the trees once more and stared intently at the car.

This time there were two people in the back. John strained his eyes to see. Yes, there could be no mistake. Sitting next to the dis-Honourable Yakobo Njoru was a beautiful, smiling woman whose face John knew only too well. Even as the car eased out into the road, John could see her leaning towards Njoru and putting her arm round his neck. There could be no doubt now. Rose had abandoned him for someone else.

She has betrayed me, he thought. After all I've done for her, all I've spent on her. After all the good times we've spent together.

He thumped his fist against the bark of the tree where he had been waiting and repeated the word, "Why, why, why?" again and again. But there was no answer, and no one to answer his question. There was only a misty memory in John's mind that in the past he had treated girlfriends in the same way as Rose had treated him, but somehow his own conduct had never seemed like betrayal because such relationships, in his view, had never been serious. And anyway, he was a man.

There was no thought in John's mind that he had contributed to the breakup. No awareness that he had become increasingly irritable and moody since his Permanent Secretary had "recruited" him. No admission that the pressure to escape his debts had cast a long shadow over his treatment of Rose.

By the time John got back to his car, anger had replaced self-pity. "What the hell!" he said to himself. "I've just been unlucky. But she's not the only fish in the sea. And when that overpaid slug of a government minister kicks her out of his beautiful mansion, she will realise what a mistake she's made. She'd better not waste any tears on me. No way! Rose Kimaga, I'm finished with you – for ever!"

He started the engine and sped down Panorama Road. The twilight was already far advanced but he didn't bother to turn on his headlights. At the bottom of the hill, he turned left into the dual carriageway that led back to the city centre. He was driving fast; too fast for the conditions.

The roads were thick with evening rush hour traffic and John was weaving his car through tight gaps. He wasn't sure where he was heading but he felt driven by the need for speed.

He shot through traffic lights that had already changed to red, ignoring the blasting horns of angry drivers. However, the traffic was turning into a jam and John could not bear being boxed in. He saw a side road that looked free of traffic and decided to do a sudden left turn, failing to notice the no entry sign.

Too late he realised he was driving the wrong way down a one-way street. A second or two later he was staring at the front of a large van coming straight towards him. Desperately, he swung the steering wheel to his left and then tensed himself for the inevitable impact.

SIX

Zeke Reappears

There was no impact.

John's car squealed to a stop at an acute angle to the white van, with no more than a centimetre between the two vehicles. John remained seated in his car, foot hard down on the brake pedal, hands gripping the steering wheel, heart pounding. "That was too close for comfort," he said aloud, and let his hands release their grip.

Before he had time to recover, the van driver had jumped down from his vehicle and rushed across to John's car, wrenching open the driver's door. He was swearing at John, who recoiled in surprise.

"You damn fool, you crazy lunatic, are you too stupid to understand a No Entry sign?"

For a few moments John felt glued to his seat, unable to respond.

"I don't know why they let crazy kids like you on the road," continued the van driver. "You could have killed someone – do you realise that?" His voice was becoming louder and more aggressive.

John mumbled a reply: "I'm sorry. I just made a mistake..."

"A mistake you call it! Get out and let me have a look at you!" the van driver shouted.

By this time, a young man had emerged from the front of the van and was making his way towards the Toyota. John briefly turned his attention away from the man, who seemed intent on starting a fight, and immediately recognised Zeke Ochieng's face.

"Zeke? Is that you, Zeke?"

"What the...? John! John Ouma!"

"You two know each other?" queried the van driver in surprise, reining back his anger.

"Yeah, we do," replied Zeke. "We're old school friends from Luboga College."

"You ought to choose your friends more carefully, Zeke. This idiot nearly killed us all. Anyway, I'm going to check that the other four in the back of the van are all right. If I stay here, I'm likely to rearrange this boy's face! Don't spend too long talking to this half-wit. We're running late, remember."

The driver turned on his heels. John meanwhile had got out of his car, and stood by the open door, staring sheepishly at Zeke.

"I'm sorry about this, Zeke. Lapse of concentration. Stupid of me."

Zeke reached out to shake his former school friend's hand. "Anyway, John, it's good to see you. How are things with you?"

"Fine. Just fine."

"You still working at the Ministry of Finance?"

"Ministry of Technology actually. Yeah, it's going well. I got promoted a while ago. How about you? Still aiming to be a teacher?"

"Yes, I've nearly finished my second year. I'm enjoying the course. And guess what? I did some teaching practice at our old school."

John smiled. "Good old Luboga College! But I can't imagine you at the front of the class."

"Neither could I a couple of years ago."

"What's this van for, Zeke?" John asked, hearing noises from the back of the vehicle.

"I'm in a band – we call ourselves the Gospel Bravos. Just in our spare time, of course. Most of the group – friends from college – are in the back of the van, with all our gear."

"I hope they're all right. I feel really bad about..."

"That's OK John. I'm getting a thumbs-up from our bass guitarist. That means: no harm done." Zeke paused, as if he was weighing up his next words. "You ought to come and hear us play."

"You still singing religious stuff?"

"Yeah, it's all Christian songs, but it's not your conventional church or gospel music. We write most of our own material. A lot of it is really down-to-earth. I think you'd like it. Might even make you think about 'religious stuff', as you call it."

"I doubt that, Zeke – but I do remember your guitar playing at school. I really admired your ability." By now the van driver was back in his seat, having checked that all was well in the back of the vehicle. He pressed his horn and waved to Zeke impatiently.

Zeke reached inside his back pocket and brought out a flyer, advertising the "Battle of the Bands" concert at the Central Park Stadium. "Here, John, take this. We're performing at the music festival in a few weeks' time. It'd be great if you can come and hear us in action. Must go now or we're going to be late for tonight's performance at the Cathedral Hall."

John took the sheet and shoved it into his back pocket. "OK, thanks, Zeke. You never know, I might find time to be there. Sorry again for the bad driving, and for delaying you. Hope your gig goes well."

They shook hands again and Zeke hurried back to the van, his thoughts once more on the gig.

As soon as the van moved away, John got back in his car, did a three-point turn and followed them out on to the main highway. In the dense traffic, he soon lost sight of the van and headed in the direction of his lodgings. As he drove he was wondering how Zeke Ochieng had managed to remain a committed Christian after leaving the safe surroundings of school life. It seemed strange to him. Maybe he would go and hear Zeke's band play at the stadium concert. But these thoughts were soon eclipsed by memories of Rose and their relationship.

John spent the rest of the week in suppressed misery. It was by now well known in his department that he had been dumped by his girl. There was no open mockery when he was present. But even through his closed office door he could hear his colleagues laughing about the misfortune of their senior accounts clerk. To his friends, John did his best to keep up an air of nonchalance, pretending that the loss of Rose made no practical difference to him. "We were getting tired of each other, anyway. So the break-up was a bit of a relief really," he told one friend, who grinned in disbelief.

His evenings were increasingly spent alone in his lodgings. And, although he would deny this to anyone who asked, he was now drinking heavily, not just beer, as in the past, but also the powerful local gin distilled from bananas. It helped him forget his problems for a while. He couldn't get out of his head the thought that he had been lied to and betrayed. He blamed Rose for his mood of depression. He even blamed her for getting him involved in corrupt activities at work.

"If it hadn't been for Rose and her expensive ways," he tried to convince himself, "I would not have needed to boost my income. I could've refused to do what the Permanent Secretary asked." With such logic John managed to deflect the blame away from himself. He only blamed himself for becoming so dependent on one girl, and for being so upset at losing her.

John couldn't shake off the mood of depression that had engulfed him. His self-respect was shattered, and the old Ouma confidence was gone. He recalled his old self before he came to the city: so full of expectation, bubbling with energy, making friends laugh at his clever jokes. Now he could not even force a smile from his own mouth.

And behind his present dark mood lurked his fears concerning the Corruption Commission. Rumour had it that the next ministry to be examined was his own, the Ministry of Technology. Again and again John wondered how well he had covered his tracks and how closely the members of the commission would examine his files.

One day merged into the next. John longed for the weekend to arrive, when he would be able to drink himself senseless and not worry about waking up for work the following morning. On the Thursday the rumours were confirmed. The Corruption Commission would definitely be in the building the next week, and everyone in the Ministry of Technology had to "be on their best behaviour" according to a memo sent round to all departments. John examined and re-examined the computer and hard-copy files related to the Masinu Diamond Mine project. *Surely*, he tried to convince himself, *nobody but a computer wizard could prove that I did anything wrong?*

He recalled that the maximum penalty for corruption was now 25 years in prison. He reflected that he could more easily endure the loss of Rose than 25 years in jail. In prison there would be no female companionship at all – but if he stayed free he could get himself another girl at any time.

John determined to break free from his self-pitying isolation. Leaving work on the Friday evening, he decided, "Tonight I am going to find myself a girl and enjoy myself!"

SEVEN

To Hell and Back

At nine o'clock that Friday night, John parked his car opposite the Kirikiri nightclub. He got out of his car, locked the doors and looked across the road. Flashing coloured lights spelt out the name Kirikiri above the entrance. He could feel the throb of the music from where he stood. But he hesitated on the kerbside and felt none of the anticipation that he would normally feel on entering the place.

For several seconds he stood with his back to his car, making no attempt to cross the road. It seemed all wrong for him to be entering the Kirikiri on his own, without Rose by his side. And what would the regulars say to him? They would ask, *Where's your lovely Rose?* And what would he say in reply? No, he couldn't face all that, even though he had primed himself with a few drinks after work. Besides, the Kirikiri wasn't the sort of place you could easily pick up a girl just for a night's pleasure, even though he and Rose had first met there.

John fumbled in his jacket pocket for his car key and turned his back on the bright lights of the nightclub. Before getting back in his car he glanced at the other vehicles along the roadside and his attention was suddenly focused on a large cream-coloured Mercedes Benz. He felt a tightening in his throat and for a moment he thought he was going to choke. The thought of Yakobo Njoru dancing with Rose in the Kirikiri nightclub filled him with a sickening sense of rage and disgust.

As soon as he could breathe easily again, John got into his car and drove away. Once again he was speeding in busy traffic. He wanted to smash something, to do something violent. He drove like someone being pursued by the police, but only his frustration and wish to escape were in pursuit.

John drove almost in a trance until at last he slowed down and brought his car to a halt in a dark street which he did not recognise. He knew he was some way east of the city centre but the surroundings were not familiar, and the street lamps – if there were any – were not working. It was dark but he could make out the familiar image of happy African faces on a Mob-Tel Network poster on a roadside hoarding. He opened his window and called to a passer-by, "What is this place?"

"If you don't know, mister, you shouldn't be here!" came the mocking reply. "This is Sikenyi suburb."

Sikenyi! John knew of the place's reputation, though he had never visited the area. It was sometimes known as the black hole of Kamobi: an area of shacks and shanty dwellings that sprawled across two sides of a valley sloping down to the polluted river known as the Drain. Sikenyi had its own community, its own commercial life, more or less independent of downtown Kamobi. Visitors from outside came here mainly for two things: alcohol and prostitutes. There was little else to attract a stranger. There were no street lights, no proper drainage and most of the roads were potholed tracks. John looked away to his right at the randomly scattered lights of the dwellings on one side of the valley. And among those lights were the red ones, offering pleasure to anyone who liked to spice his pleasure with a hint of risk.

Rumours abounded about those who had disappeared after visiting Sikenyi at night, and John had heard that the occasional unidentified body was found at daybreak, laid out on the side of an open rubbish heap. But, he reflected, rumours often exaggerated the truth. From where he stood, the place looked harmless enough.

He could hear the lively babble of innumerable drinking parties. It reminded him of home, friendly gatherings round a fire at night, when traditional stories could be shared and locally brewed beer could be enjoyed. The old ways are not all bad, he thought. He continued to gaze at the scattered lights and, instead of sensing danger, he felt the warmth of companionship. He said to himself: *No one will recognise me here. Here a man can forget his worries and lose his identity.*

He removed his jacket and threw it on the back seat. Best not to look too smart in this place, John reflected, as he locked the car and began walking down a dirt track towards a sign that read Pombe Bar. Before he had reached the bar he could smell the tang of locally brewed beer. That's what I need, he thought — real beer, not the synthetic taste of bottled lager.

He entered the bar and nervously looked around at the

people already present. Some of them eyed him suspiciously and their conversation grew quieter. He wondered if any of them were thieves, and felt glad that he was not carrying much money with him. He found a dark corner and rested his elbows on the creaking table. A large cockroach sneaked into a crack in the wall behind John's chair, where the plaster was crumbling away from the earth. No smoking ban was maintained here, and a swirl of cigarette smoke clung to the ceiling boards. From outside came the voice of women gathered round the great pots in which the bananas were being brewed.

"You want bottled beer? Or we can serve our own pombe in a pot with a straw," the bar owner asked John.

"You brew it round the back?" asked John.

"We do. And it's good – the real thing. But be warned: we brew it strong."

John smiled. "That's exactly what I need. Strong, traditional beer."

A minute later a small pot, full of pombe, together with a wide drinking straw, was brought to him, and John settled down to his drink. He noticed that the conversation of the other drinkers had again become loud and animated, and nobody seemed to be paying him any attention now.

As he drank, his worries quietly dissolved. His sense of failure slowly disappeared from his mind, and he began to feel at peace with the world.

He ordered more pombe as soon as he had finished his first pot. He could not grasp why he had felt so miserable during the week. He didn't need Rose Kimaga, after all; and as for the Corruption Commission, they were all too stupid to detect his clever and brilliant fraud. Who cared about them anyway?

He could now understand that there was no reason to be depressed. John recalled the words of a song that he had heard at the Kirikiri – *Life is here to be enjoyed: what are you worrying for?* Exactly so. The song said it all! Life is here for enjoyment. John sucked through his straw, and the pombe seemed to work magic in his soul as it diffused through his body.

By the time John was half-way through his third pot his vision was becoming slightly blurred. He wasn't entirely sure where he was, but he felt good and suddenly announced to the other drinkers: "They can't touch me, you know. I am far too clever. And I am not worried."

Some of the other customers cheered him sarcastically. They could tell when a man was not used to the local brew. One man called out, "You may not be worried now. But later? Ha ha ha!" A ripple of laughter ran through the room. Then everyone turned back to their conversations and left John to his solitary drinking session.

A woman in a tight-fitting top appeared from an inner room and quietly walked up to the table where John was seated. She pulled up her short skirt, sat down and stared into John's face. "Would you like to buy me a drink, handsome?"

John opened his eyes wide and for a second wondered if Rose was speaking to him. He realised his mistake and stuttered, "My pleasure. Wh-what will you have?" He rose clumsily to his feet, almost losing his balance.

"It's OK, I'll get it from the bar." She soon returned

with a glass of coke, and once again sat down and stared with wide eyes into John's face.

John reminded himself of what he had planned to do – apart from getting drunk. "You know," he said, "when I look at you, I think to myself: that is a woman."

"You are very observant."

"No, I mean a real woman. I mean the sort of woman who knows how to treat a man properly. How to give a man what he wants."

"And what does a man want?"

"You know what a man wants." John leaned forward and took hold of her left hand, which he began to stroke with his thumb.

"Perhaps I do," she replied coyly.

"And you wouldn't treat a man badly, would you?"

"You've been treated badly?"

"Very, very badly."

"Sorry to hear that – er, what's your name?"

"My name is John. And I am the S-senior Acc-accounts C-clerk at the M-ministry of Tech-techno-technogy." John was vaguely aware that some of his words weren't coming out right, but the girl didn't seem to mind.

"I am impressed, John. You must handle a lot of money in your work."

"Of course I can handle money. I am very good at handling money!"

The woman withdrew her hand from John's. "I am glad to hear that, John, because, you know, my services are not cheap."

John stared into the deep dark eyes of the other and thought he had found a long lost treasure. "Cheap? You are too beautiful to be cheap. Look, I can afford to pay for a real woman like you." John had taken out his wallet from his trouser pocket and was about to pull out some banknotes.

The woman placed her hand firmly over his and whispered, "Not here, John. I have a nice place in the next street. It's really close. We can talk business when we get there. Just leave enough money for your drinks. Come on, let's go."

John found that his head was swimming and he struggled to keep his balance once he was on his feet. The woman put one arm round his waist to steady him and guided him slowly to the door. John leaned on her for support. He had lost track of how much alcohol he had consumed since leaving his office that evening. The other drinkers watched their slow progress and exchanged knowing looks.

Before they left the bar, the woman looked over her shoulder and nodded to two men who were sitting in a shadowy alcove to one side of the bar.

Outside, John and the woman made their way slowly and clumsily round a corner into a dark alleyway. John was murmuring, "You are a real woman. A real woman. But please tell me your name."

Abruptly she took her arm from him and, without her support, he sank to his knees. The woman replied in a harsh tone, "You don't need to know my name, Mister Senior Accounts Clerk. OK boys, he's all yours." She called to two figures concealed within the darkness of the alley.

The next thing that John knew was a crashing impact as a booted foot landed on the side of his head. The kick sent him floundering to the ground. Instinctively he tried to roll himself into a ball, but the hammer blows of fists and feet rained down on him without mercy, without pause, until, finally, an explosive crunch to his skull sent him into oblivion.

* * * * *

He was in a deep hollow in the earth and the diamonds were sparkling all around him. He reached upwards towards the seam where the nearest diamonds lay embedded, but his fingers could not grip onto anything, and he beat his fists on the rock face in frustration and fury. Then he heard a deep throbbing from the surrounding earth and the ground beneath his feet shook. Earth and rocks were tumbling down from above, building up to a deadly landslide. He looked upwards to the diminishing light, shielding his face from the impact of the falling debris. He tried to scramble up the steep side of the great pit, yet after every desperate step he slipped back. Nowhere could he find a secure grip. He was going to be buried alive under a thousand tons of falling rock and earth. There was a drumming in his ears, coming from all directions, and the sound was becoming louder and louder so that he wanted to scream *stop!* But he could not utter one word for when he parted his lips slimy soil filled his mouth.

The drumming carried on, unremitting, thumping into his brain, and now it was joined by a hysterical voice screaming out a song: it was a song that his friend Zeke Ochieng used to sing but now it was distorted by hateful mockery:

> You can gain the whole wide world, my friend, and lose
>   your very soul;
> And when you die what do you get?
> A coffin and a small rectangular hole!

The voice ended in cracked laughter, while the drumming increased in volume, until it was inside his head, hammering on his temples, threatening to split his brain apart, until at last he groaned aloud and opened his eyes painfully. Consciousness trickled back into his mind. He became aware of his surroundings. He was lying on the ground, in a depression that smelt like an open sewer. Sikenyi. Of course.

A repulsive mixture of vile smells hit him and he retched, spewing up much of the drink he had consumed the night before. With slow, painful effort, he sat up. As soon as he did so, his head jerked forward as he vomited once more. The thumping he had heard in his semi-conscious state did not come from a drum, but from a violent headache that seemed to be about to burst his head open. His whole body was throbbing with the pain of multiple bruising. He knew what a hangover was like, but this physical agony was like nothing he had experienced before.

For several minutes he sat there, unable to move, unable even to open his eyes except for a moment. Finally, he looked up, forcing his eyes to remain open. He was sitting next to a rubbish heap: piles of bottles, paper and rotting food had been dumped on a piece of waste ground. To one side there was a storm drain, oozing foul water and sewage. The eastern horizon was beginning to lighten with the morning sun. He could hear the droning of distant traffic, but no sounds came to him from nearby. He felt inside his pockets for his wallet, but his pockets were empty. His watch, his phone, his wallet were all gone. He had been robbed of everything but his clothes. He looked down at his feet: they had even taken his shoes.

"What – what happened?" he croaked, gripped by a sudden wave of panic. Then he remembered: the bar, the pombe, the woman leading him to somewhere but never arriving and the assault from the shadows – the rain of hammer blows on his head and body until everything had gone black. . .

He struggled to his feet. The smell of vomit and sewage struck him like a physical blow, and it seemed like his head was spinning off his body. He stood for a while until his vision cleared. He looked round at his surroundings but could not determine where he was in relation to the bar where he had been drinking. But he could see that he was down in the Sikenyi valley and needed to make his way up the slope to the road where he had left his car.

He staggered slowly along the nearest track leading up the valley side. His socks were being cut and ripped on the rough surface but he hardly noticed the pain from his feet, when so much of his body was hurting. With every step the pounding in his head doubled its strength so that his whole body was wet with sweat by the time he reached the road skirting the top of the valley.

He looked around for his red Toyota among the clapped-out cars and pick-ups that lined the road. He couldn't see it anywhere. Then he remembered that he had left his car by a roadside hoarding advertising the Mob-Tel phone network.

He made slow, painful progress along the road, passing a few walkers who looked at him suspiciously but said nothing. Finally, he could see the hoarding with its happy faces celebrating the joys of being connected to Mob-Tel.

He scanned the vehicles around but there was no red Toyota. And then he remembered: empty pockets! Of course, they had taken his keys. The thieves would have driven his car to a safe hiding place where they would quickly alter the identity with new paint and a new registration number. There would be nothing to show that the car belonged to John Ouma, apart from the chassis number – but who would bother to check such details? Certainly not the police: they had far more important things to attend to.

So they've taken my car too, John thought with hopeless resignation. He had no choice but to keep walking. He wondered why people stared at him, moving out of his way, as though he was contaminated with some nameless disease. He did not realise what a mess he looked, and his sense of smell had grown accustomed to the stench which clung to his clothes and body.

He turned round and looked at the sprawling community of Sikenyi. The place looked strangely innocent now, with the smoke of its cooking-fires curling peacefully upwards into the sky. But John had the feeling that he was walking away from the jaws of hell.

EIGHT

Mr Mwive
Shows His Hand

Somehow John managed to get back to his rooms later that morning. He had a vague memory of a kind motorcyclist agreeing to take him to the nearest police station, where he reported the theft of his car and possessions. The police sergeant on duty was unsympathetic when he heard that John had visited a bar in Sikenyi at night. "You can say goodbye to your car and everything else that was taken," he said. "I hope you've learnt a lesson, Mr Ouma. They might have killed you, you know."

John wasn't sure about learning any lesson – except that painkillers only relieved some of the pain from being beaten up. From the police station he was able to phone a friend who collected him in his car and drove him to his lodgings. The rest of the weekend was spent in bed, or in the bathroom being sick. John wondered how he would be able to drag himself to work on Monday; he also worried about how he would break the news about his car to his uncle, to whom he still owed a good part of the loan. He had taken out only basic insurance on his car, so the insurers would not compensate him for his loss. His car-owning days were over for a long time.

On Sunday he went for a short walk, gritting his teeth through the occasional surges of pain. He wondered whether the smell of the beer, of the rubbish tip, of urine and sewage had been completely washed off his body, and the memory of his visit to Sikenyi was still strong in his mind. He felt conspicuous: a young man shuffling along like an ancient village elder. His face was bloated from the blows he had received, and he had two broken teeth. At least, to his amazement, he had no broken bones.

He bought a copy of the Sunday edition of the *Kamobi Reporter* and read the headline: CABINET PURGE EXPECTED. The news centred on the activities of the Corruption Commission. Most of the article was speculation, but the gist of the news was that a number of high officials, even members of the cabinet, could be sacked and even brought to trial on charges of corrupt use of public funds. The editorial in the paper questioned which government ministries were first in the queue, but John knew that his own, the Ministry of Technology, was ear-marked for the Commission's scrutiny in the weeks ahead.

As far as John was concerned, it was only his own ministry – and more particularly his own job security – that mattered. He thought about the imposing, self-assured figure of Mr Mwive, his Permanent Secretary. And he knew that when big men fell, little men usually fell with them. If Mr Mwive was exposed as corrupt, then he would be lucky to escape investigation. So he hoped, for his own sake, that his Permanent Secretary was safe from arrest.

He was allowed to take the next week off work, to give him some time to recover, but the days dragged heavily on John, with no Rose to keep him company and little spare cash to spend. He wondered what was happening at Min-tech, whether members of the Commission had arrived in the accounts department, whether they were already going through his files. During the week, having acquired a cheap phone from an illegal street seller, he phoned his office and, to his surprise, was put through to the Permanent Secretary.

"Ah, John," said Mr Mwive, in a sympathetic tone, "I was very sorry to hear about your – your accident."

"Thank you, sir. It was hardly an accident. I got beaten up."

"Yes, yes, I heard. Most unfortunate. But you are recovering, I hope?"

"I am. Slowly. I still get these bad headaches, but I hope to be fit for work next week."

"Good. Good. Please call at my office when you come."

"Thank you, sir, I shall. May I ask something?"

There was an awkward pause, as if Mr Mwive did not wish to hear the question. At last, he replied: "Of course. Ask anything you want."

"The Commission, sir. Is it. . . ? Has it. . . ?"

"Has it what, John?"

"Has it begun its work? Are they in the building?"

The Permanent Secretary chuckled in his throat. "Oh, yes, they are around, but there's nothing to worry about.

Just enjoy your break from work. You'll find out everything when you come in on Monday. Goodbye."

The line went dead, before John could respond. The words of his P.S. seemed to be reassuring, so John experienced some relief from his worries. By the following weekend, the aching of his bones had reduced, and he felt able to face work once again. Some of his old confidence had returned. He could dream of enjoying life once more, with the hopes of finding a new girlfriend and future promotion at work. The Corruption Commission would soon be a distant memory.

However, when he went to work the following Monday, his hopes came crashing down on his head. He arrived at his office to find Wilson Sembatya occupying his desk in the room of the Senior Accounts Clerk.

John restrained his annoyance and said, "OK, Wilson, I'm back now. You can go back to your desk."

Wilson made no attempt to move from his seat. "It's not like that, John. You see, I've been. . . ."

"Yeah, thanks for filling in for me, but now you can get out of my chair."

As John moved angrily towards his colleague, Wilson rose from his seat, backed away and stood looking sardonically at John, who sat down and typed in his password.

"What are you waiting for?" John asked.

"You'll see." Wilson continued to stand, with his arms folded, a smirk on his lips.

John stared at the screen: Access denied. Password not recognised. He retyped his password, this time more carefully.

The same message was repeated. He tried a third time with the same result.

"What the hell's wrong with this? I bet the I.T. department have messed things up again."

"It's not the I.T. department, John. Why don't you ask the P.S.?"

John looked up at Wilson, who seemed to know what was going on.

"What's this all about, Wilson?"

"As I say, the Permanent Secretary can explain things better than me."

John recalled Mr Mwive's words on the phone – that John should call in at his office on his return to work.

Two minutes later he was in the office of the P.S., staring once more into those deep shadowy eyes and feeling the same insecurity that he had felt before when talking to this powerful man.

"Excuse me, sir, but for some reason, my password has been blocked."

Mr Mwive did not reply, his eyes widening as if he needed more explanation.

"And I need it to be unblocked so I can get down to work."

"That won't be necessary, Mr Ouma," came the reply.

"What – what do you mean, sir?"

The P.S. took out an envelope from his desk drawer and handed it to John.

"What's this?"

"Open it. Read it. It will explain everything."

The envelope had the name J.A. OUMA neatly printed on it. He tore it open and took out the letter, which was printed on official Min-tech notepaper. John felt confused but forced himself to concentrate on the text:

Dear Mr Ouma,

We regret to inform you that your work as Senior Accounts Clerk, and previously as Assistant Accounts Clerk, has not attained an adequate level of performance, and, in spite of several opportunities given you to improve your efficiency, no significant progress has been observed. Targets have not been met.

Lack of dedication and a decreasing commitment to your duties have meant that the financial affairs of the Ministry have been left in a state of some disarray. Moreover, it has been noted that a number of irregularities have occurred in your accounts, none of which have been adequately explained.

It is therefore with regret that I have no alternative but to dismiss you from your post at this Ministry with immediate effect. Your salary will be paid up to the end of this month. I wish you success in your future employment.

Yours sincerely
Y.W. MWIVE
Permanent Secretary

John stared at the letter as though stupefied. He couldn't take it in and thought there must be some mistake; or maybe some ill-judged practical joke was being played on him. But the man of the other side of the desk was not smiling, merely studying John's face like a psychiatrist watching a patient.

Finally, John spoke, in a voice that trembled with emotion: "You're firing me?"

"You can see what the letter says. It's your own failures that have led to the termination of your appointment. It's not up to me to fire or hire you."

"What failures, Mr Mwive? Tell me! What are my inadequacies? I've worked in this place for over two years without a complaint!"

The Permanent Secretary was unmoved by the rising tide of anger in John's voice. His reply was calm and deliberate. "Mr Ouma, I am not here to argue with you. I am merely informing you of the situation."

"What situation? You refer in the letter to unexplained 'irregularities' in my accounting. You mean the corrupt deals that I have helped you to arrange?"

The word "corrupt" seemed to disperse Mr Mwive's placid mood. He rose to his feet and spoke in a voice of outrage and indignation.

"Corrupt! How dare you accuse me of such conduct? How dare you speak to me in that way? Have you forgotten who I am? And who you are?"

The Permanent Secretary's anger was matched by John's. "Yes, I know who you are, Mister Big Shot Permanent Secretary. And I know you now for what you are: a corrupt, lying, manipulating hypocrite!"

"I think you'd better leave immediately before I have you arrested."

"Arrested for what, Mr Mwive? Arrested for being your fixer in your money-grabbing frauds?"

"You're out of your mind, Ouma!"

John stabbed his index finger towards the other man and leant across the desk in a threatening manner. "Really? Is it just coincidence that you're sacking me just when the Corruption Commission might be sniffing the bad smells you've left in the air?"

"I don't have to listen to your raving, Ouma." Mr Mwive pressed a button on his intercom and shouted: "Send security in here – immediately!"

The word "security" caused John to pause in his verbal assault. He stood back from the desk, lowered his right hand and said quietly, "I'll take my story to the Press, Mwive. I'll expose you."

"And who will believe you? And are you going to confess to all your own criminal activity? You are talking like a fool."

The next moment a blue-uniformed security guard barged into the room, a rifle grasped in both hands, ready for action. The P.S. spoke to him calmly, burying his fury at John's rudeness. "I want you to accompany this gentleman here out of the building. He is not to enter any of the offices on his way out. Please make sure he does not linger outside the Ministry. Is that clear?"

"Yes, sir. Out of building. Not enter rooms. Not to linger."

"Goodbye, Ouma. I'm sure your talents will be appreciated elsewhere," Mr Mwive said to John as the guard guided him forcibly out of the office. John did not reply but screwed up the letter of dismissal and tossed it on the floor of the office before the door closed behind him.

Back at his lodgings John sat on his bed, his chin cupped in his hands, struggling to absorb what had happened to him that morning. His brain was fizzing with questions. How had he been so led by the nose? Why had he agreed to assist in corruption in the first place? How had he been such a fool as to trust the poisonous "friendship" of a man like Mwive?

He realised all too clearly why he had been dismissed from his job. He knew too much. He had had access to a number of files, including the recent one relating to the diamond mine project — files which would point unmistakably to the Permanent Secretary's guilt. It was much safer for Mwive to have John off the scene permanently. And, as for revenge, John knew there was no chance of getting his own back on Mwive. No newspaper or magazine would publish his allegations for fear of reprisals from the government; and, even if they did, the story would expose him as a fraudster, too. He was a sacrifice on the altar of Mwive's wellbeing and there was absolutely nothing he could do about it. He raged against the injustice of what was happening to him. He raged, too, against his feelings of powerlessness.

And then John pondered the consequences of his situation: no job, no income, no means of paying his bills, no prospect of another job — unless, perhaps, he could get a letter of recommendation from the Ministry, which seemed unlikely in the circumstances.

"What a fool I've been!" he moaned. "They've thrown

me out. They threw old Molo out and now it's my turn. And I bet it'll be Wilson Sembatya's turn next!"

There was no relief from John's self-disgust except in the bottle of gin at his bedside. The spirits gradually eased his mind until he drifted into a shallow sleep tortured by images of suffocation in a collapsing mine shaft.

NINE

Escape Plan

The following day, partly hung over from the previous day's drinking, John made his way to the city park and watched the weaver birds busily constructing their hanging nests in the trees that lined the perimeter. The spherical nests were small miracles of interwoven twigs and stems. The nest building was accompanied by a chorus of excited twittering. The birds' purposeful activity reminded John of his own lack of purpose and, instead of cheering him, it deepened his mood of grim resignation.

He thought of phoning home. He had not spoken to his mother for months, and he felt guilty about this neglect, especially as his father had passed away the year before. He took out his new phone and began to tap out the number, but then he stopped. He replaced the phone in his pocket. He couldn't speak to her in his present circumstances: it would only mean more lying and pretending. He had to find a way of escape from his pit of failure before he could consider speaking to the family back in Mkandu village.

He dragged himself back to his rooms, without any

plan except to buy himself another bottle from his rapidly disappearing supply of cash. He was well aware that his bank account had almost run dry. On reaching the end of his street, he was surprised to see the short, squat figure of his landlord waiting outside his apartment block and looking intently in his direction.

"Good morning, Mr Ouma."

"Morning, Mr Mali. How are you?"

"Personally I am fine, but I wonder how you are?"

"Why should you wonder?"

"Well, it seems you are having trouble."

"Yeah, I was beaten up the other week. But I'm feeling OK now."

"I wasn't thinking of that, Mr Ouma, although I am pleased to hear you have recovered. I was thinking of the trouble you seem to have in paying your rent."

In all his worries, this was one that John had pushed to the back of his mind: the fact that he was three months behind with his rent. He had ignored the reminders that had been sent to him. Other matters had seemed more important.

"Yes, I'm sorry about that, Mr Mali. I'll see to it at the end of this month."

"That's not good enough. Here, take this." He handed John a sealed envelope.

John's heartbeat surged as he remembered a similar scene at Mr Mwive's office the day before. "What's this?" he asked.

"It's a notice to quit."

"You – you're asking me to leave?"

"No, not *asking* you: *telling* you. You must leave these rooms, so I can offer them to someone who'll pay their rent."

"Give me a few more days, Mr Mali. Please. I get paid at the end of the month."

"Maybe you will, maybe you won't," said the landlord, looking at his tenant with sceptical eyes. "But you don't seem to be at your office, as I would expect at this time in the morning. What's happened? Have you lost your job?"

"None of your business."

"Fair enough – my only business is to collect the rent. You've had enough warnings in the past. You ignored them, so now I want you out of here unless you can pay all the rent you owe today."

"Please, Mr Mali, just a few days."

"It's too late for all these delaying tactics. Pay up today or get out today."

"That's impossible."

"That's up to you. Mr Ouma. I shall be back in the evening, at around seven o'clock. If you haven't got the rent, you'd better be gone. And make sure you leave the keys with a neighbour." The landlord paused, as if he wished to remember something. "Oh yes, and I shall bring some friends with me, just to make sure you'll make no trouble."

John said in a tone of bitter resentment, "You are just like the rest, aren't you?"

The landlord spat on the ground at John's feet. "I don't know what you mean by that. I'm not like anyone else except myself. And, anyway, I don't give a damn what you think of me. You have two choices: pay your rent or clear out." He pointed to the letter in John's hand, and added, "Read it at your leisure. It's all official. You've got a few hours! Remember, seven o'clock. That's your deadline."

He turned round and strode away, leaving his tenant speechless. John sat down wearily on the front step at the entrance of the apartment block. He gazed with unfocused vision at the people passing busily by on the pavement. He murmured: "What am I going to do now? I've lost my girlfriend, lost my car, my job – and now I have nowhere to live. This is more than I can stand."

There was a deep quivering in his heart. It seemed that his normal heartbeat had been replaced by a lighter, quicker, racing rhythm. He thought, even my body is going out of control.

John continued to sit on the step until his heartbeat finally settled to its usual rhythm. He put his arms round his legs and rested his head on his knees. "Why? Why? Why?" he kept repeating, but there was no one who took any notice and there was nobody to provide him with an answer.

John spent the rest of the day wandering aimlessly round the side-streets of the city, occasionally stopping at a bar for a drink.

The man renting the rooms opposite his had kindly agreed to look after John's things until he could collect them, so John had hastily stuffed his possession into a few bags and boxes and handed them over.

"I'll collect them later in the week," he said, but he wondered whether he would bother. His range of smart shirts and ties seemed of little value now.

During his wanderings, John tried to analyse his circumstances. His life, he reckoned, had become a list of negatives, but there was little point in blaming others. For example, there was his landlord, Mr Mali – a man whom John heartily despised; but who was to blame for the three months' unpaid rent? Not his landlord, surely. It was the fault of no one else but John Ouma.

He sat down in a bar near the central bus park and ordered a vodka.

The buses were roaring past on their way to upcountry towns and villages. For a while he considered taking one of the buses to his home area and seeing his mother and the rest of the family in Mkandu. He had enough money for the bus fare – so why not?

He knew why not. Pride. He couldn't go back in his present state and face humiliation. He was the first in his family to reach A-level standard at school, and he was regarded as a trailblazer for his younger siblings. He couldn't go back empty-handed. He recalled his clever pun on the name of his village –*Mkandu. Me-Can-Do.* It sounded like a sick joke now.

It seemed almost incredible to John that, within such a short space of time – a handful of days – he had lost everything that had made life enjoyable and worthwhile. But it was no use looking back to the past, no matter how recent; even yesterday was out-of-date. Today was what counted.

As he drank a second vodka, his mind seemed to become clearer. He felt he could look at himself more honestly than ever before. And the thing that seemed clearer than anything else was this: he had no future. He was like a village house battered by a tornado – roof gone, walls cracked and crumbling, rubble scattered around. There was only one

98

thing to do with such a wreck: pull it down completely. As for rebuilding, that wasn't part of John's plans.

When he left the bar, having drunk a third vodka, dusk was beginning to fall. It would soon be dark. A strange calm had come into John's mind. Now that he had decided on a definite course of action, a quiet resolve took hold of him, and he felt more certain of himself than he had been for many days.

He crossed the road and walked along the outside of the perimeter wall that enclosed the bus park. He observed how the buses, once they had driven through the exit and turned into Aggrey Avenue, accelerated away regardless of the pedestrians and motorcyclists. He recalled how he had sometimes seen accidents from his office window on the third floor of the Ministry of Technology block. People did not usually survive being struck by a bus in full flight.

John walked determinedly along Aggrey Avenue to the point where the buses seemed to reach their maximum speed before having to brake prior to reaching the road junction further on. There were no pedestrian crossings here and, anyway, these were disregarded by most drivers in Kamobi. Pedestrians raced across the road in the gaps between oncoming vehicles. You had to have your wits about you to survive on foot in the mad chaotic roads of the city.

John paused at the kerbside. He watched a bus turning the corner on his left and roaring down the road until it passed him at 50 kph or more. He thought to himself, that will do surely? He wished he had a pen or pencil so he could write some sort of message, but what message did he have to send? *Sorry, mother. Sorry for being such a failure and letting you down.* Yes: that would be the most appropriate. But it was too late for that now.

In the west the sky was red with the dying sun, and slowly an oppressive greyness, growing darker every second, was beginning to cover the rest of the sky. The dusk would bring little relief from the continuing heat of the dry season.

Still, John remained standing at the kerb, steeling his will for what had to be done. And, while he stood there, greyness merged into blackness as the equatorial twilight quickly swallowed the light of day. The sunset had shrunk to a feeble purple streak on the western sky.

John found himself trembling uncontrollably, and for a moment he wondered whether he had the courage to carry out his resolve.

Another bus was leaving the bus park, turning the corner. He could hear the engine revving in low gear. He could see the bright headlights approaching as the vehicle surged down the road in his direction, gathering speed every second.

A voice within him seemed to be saying: *This is it, John! This is it!*

A decision was made.

John stepped quickly into the path of the approaching bus. The headlights dazzled his eyes; the noise of the engine filled his ears like thunder. For a fraction of a second he heard the harsh squealing of brakes, then the great vehicle was upon him. He felt no pain. Just a curtain of darkness extinguishing his mind.

TEN

Message in the Music

Even before he opened his eyes, John knew he was in a hospital. A pungent smell of bodily fluids and disinfectant was in his nostrils. He could hear voices as though far off, echoing down a corridor. He could feel softness beneath the palms of his hands. At the same time, he was aware of a dull pain filtering through his brain from some part, or parts, of his body.

He opened his eyes slowly, reluctantly. Yes, he was in a hospital ward, with beds on either side of his. Uniformed nurses were moving across his blurred vision. A sluggish ceiling fan was spinning slowly above. Unshaded light bulbs were burning feebly. Bright light was shining through curtained windows.

I'm not dead, he thought. I'm not dead – and I should be!

The memory of a huge bus bearing down on him with blazing headlights seized his imagination and he was again tensing himself for that terrible impact, which, somehow, he had never felt.

He tried to sit up, but sharp spears of pain jabbed at his body and he gave up the attempt with a groan. A nurse, alerted by this sound, hurried to his bedside. John looked questioningly at her as she felt his pulse. He was still not completely certain that what his eyes were seeing was reality rather than some mental illusion at the point of death. *Maybe I'll be dead in just a moment*, he wondered. *Maybe this is just my mind about to shut down.*

"Nurse," he croaked feebly.

"Shhh – you are too weak to talk. Just rest."

"Nurse," John persisted, "I've got to know."

"You don't have to know anything," came the soothing reply. "Just try to rest. The doctor will speak to you on his rounds later."

"What – what time is it?"

"It's nearly nine o'clock."

"What? Nine at night?"

"No, nine in the morning. Look at the sunlight coming through the windows."

"How is that possible? It was in the evening, just after sunset, that..."

"You've been unconscious. You have bad concussion. I wasn't on duty when they brought you in, but don't worry, we'll look after you." She wiped his face with a damp cloth. John felt that nobody had shown so much concern for him for a long time. She patted him on the shoulder, smiled and moved to another bed.

John mumbled under his breath: "Nine o'clock. Nine o'clock. Good grief, I've been knocked out for more than twelve hours."

Now the questions began to flood into his awakened mind. *How did I get here? Why didn't the bus kill me? Why aren't I dead for goodness sake?* And finally, *What is the point of my surviving?*

Some time later a young doctor took shape in his vision. He sat on a chair at John's bedside. "So you are back in the land of the living?"

John winced. "Is that a joke, doctor?"

"No – just a comment on the fact that you've been unconscious for a while. We weren't sure what damage that crack on the head had done. Fortunately for you it's not more serious. We will be doing a brain scan later."

"Doctor, can you tell me what happened?"

The doctor took a pen from his shirt pocket and said, "First of all, we need some personal details. You had no I.D. on you. What's your name?"

"John. It's John Ouma."

"Right, I can spell that. What about next of kin?"

John nearly choked. "Next of kin?" Suddenly it seemed that he was a candidate for death after all.

"It's OK, you're not going to die. We need to contact a relative so we can tell them you are here."

"Here? Where?"

"Mugalo Hospital. You know, the one with the tower block overlooking Central Park?"

"Yeah, of course I know." John was irritated by the fact that the next of kin in Kamobi was his uncle, the one who had provided a loan for his car – and he dreaded meeting his uncle in this situation. But John felt too weak to resist the doctor's questions and, reluctantly, he gave the information.

While the young doctor was writing down these details, John said, "There's a pain coming from my right leg. It's getting worse."

"OK, we'll give you a painkilling injection. I'm afraid we shall have to operate. You've broken your leg. Not sure how seriously. We'll find out when we take you to theatre."

"Is that all the damage? Just a broken leg?"

"Not quite. You've got a bad gash on your head. That bandage will have to be changed – blood is still oozing through. You have some nasty cuts too – they might need one or two stitches, nothing too serious. And I noticed some bruising across the ribs – but they're not new, are they?"

"No, I got those from a couple of thieves, a while ago."

"Sorry to hear that. Overall, for a man who had an argument with a bus, you have come off remarkably lightly."

"You know what happened?" John waited, in fearful anticipation, for the phrase "attempted suicide".

"Only what I've been told." The doctor looked closely at John, as though he had guessed the motives for his "accident". "Apparently, you were trying to cross Aggrey Avenue in the evening rush hour and you didn't see a bus coming in your direction."

"I thought it would kill me."

The doctor called to a passing nurse, "Nurse, can you get this bandage changed?" Then he turned back to John and regarded him quizzically. "You thought it would kill you?"

John was flustered. He hadn't chosen his words carefully. "I mean, when it struck me, I thought it was all over for me."

"Well, I've seen a few people hit by buses and lorries – and they don't usually survive. I think maybe the bus knocked you clear. The gash on your head must be from the road surface, where you landed. If the bus had run over you, you'd be in the mortuary by now."

"Thanks for being frank."

"My name's Joseph, not Frank, by the way."

John managed a weak smile at the doctor's quip, but he didn't reply.

"What I mean, John, is this. You're very lucky to be alive and to have every prospect of a full recovery. If I were you, I'd give thanks to God for preserving my life. But that's up to you. Now you must excuse me: I have other patients to see."

When the doctor had left his bedside, John turned his head and mumbled into his pillow: "Give thanks to God? Give thanks to God! What a farce! I'm a failure even in trying to end my life."

And John continued mumbling "God, God, God," into his pillow. It was almost, almost, a prayer.

* * * * *

Ten days later John discharged himself from hospital, his right leg in plaster, walking with the aid of a crutch. He could not yet put any weight upon the leg that had suffered a multiple fracture, but at least he could move around, and it seemed strange walking under a cloudless sky after being confined to a hospital ward for so many days. He felt nervous, uncertain of himself, walking along the pavement like a feeble old man.

He had no immediate plans – no plans at all, really, except to avoid staying with his uncle. Uncle Yosiah Opio had visited him in Mugalo Hospital two days after his admission there, and, when he had heard from John's lips the catalogue of disasters that had occurred, he had become unsympathetic. It was pretty obvious that he believed John's accident near the bus park was not accidental. He made it plain that he would offer John no further help. "You are on your own, John," he said. "When you leave hospital, you can come and stay with me for one night at my house in the suburbs. And then I will give you bus fare to get home to Mkandu. That's all. You get nothing more from me."

John could not blame his uncle for his attitude. He had lost a lot of money because of his nephew's failure to keep up with repayments on the car loan and now there was no prospect of John paying him back.

So, when John left the hospital, he did not contact Uncle Opio. He wanted some time, some space, first of all to think what his options were. Perhaps he would phone his uncle later. Perhaps he had no other option.

The air outside was still heavy with heat. The dry season had not given up its grip on the city, and the longed-for rains had not yet arrived. John headed for the Central Park, just a stone's throw from the hospital, and there he seated himself in the shade of a mango tree.

He found it hard to analyse his state of mind: there was a numbness, an aimlessness, a terrifying absence of ideas and feelings. He compared himself to a room emptied of all its furniture and other contents, with a voice crying, "Why? Why?" echoing from wall to wall.

Death, as a way of escape, had been denied him. One thing John had decided: he would never again attempt to take his own life. But to confront the future in his present situation was an unappealing alternative. He was no longer desperate: just resigned to existence without a clear purpose.

A discarded newspaper lying on the ground under the park bench caught his eye. The date was Friday: the day before. The headline read:

Commission Shows Its Teeth

and below the headline a sub-heading:

Min-tech Official Arrested

John scanned the text with greedy attention until he read the following words:

Yokana Mwive, Permanent Secretary at the Ministry of Technology, was taken into custody last night on suspicion of fraud and misappropriation of funds. Mr Mwive has put out a statement through his lawyer denying all allegations of corruption. It is expected that he will be formally charged tomorrow morning.

John stared, fascinated by the article. He might have expected to feel delight and even triumph at the news of Mwive's downfall. Instead he felt a deep sadness at the state of things in his country, to which he himself had contributed. He knew there were bigger fish than Mwive swimming in the same pool, and they would probably never be caught or brought to justice. John wondered if he would be pursued by the investigators. He didn't know – and, strangely, he didn't care at that moment. He thought, they can't do worse to me than I've done to myself.

"What next?" John asked himself. As if in answer to his own question, he reached inside the back pocket of his jeans and felt a screwed up piece of paper. He took it out and flattened it on the bench beside him. It was a flyer for the Battle of Bands concert at the nearby stadium:

Kamobi Musical Festival
presents
THE BATTLE OF THE BANDS
Saturday 14th March from 2 pm
featuring
Slickers at 2 pm
Afro Blasters at 2.45 pm
Gospel Bravos at 3.30 pm

John paused in his reading of the list of performers, which continued down the page. He recalled that the flyer must be the one that Zeke Ochieng had given him when he'd nearly hit the white van his band was travelling in. And he felt sure that the name of Zeke's group must be the third on the list – the Gospel Bravos.

"I'll go and listen to them," John decided. "The stadium's not far – just the other side of the park. It'll be something to do. Better than nothing."

He bought himself a meat samosa from a kiosk and set off across the park. He had no watch but, judging by the height of the sun, he reckoned it was already past two o'clock. Soon enough he could hear the dance rhythms of a band performing on a stage in the centre of the small stadium. By the time he arrived on the other side of the park, the music had stopped and another band was setting up their equipment. John paid the entrance fee from his diminishing supply of cash and sat down at the bottom of one of the stands; he wasn't going to climb the terraces with a crutch and a useless leg.

The stands were by no means full. Probably they would fill up in the evening, when perhaps the more popular bands would be playing. Nevertheless, John reckoned there were at least two thousand in the stadium when the next act, the Afro Blasters, began their set of songs.

John wasn't a big blues fan and, although the African flavour given to traditional American music appealed to him, he was really waiting to see how Zeke's group would perform. It must be nerve-racking, he pondered, playing on such a large stage.

After half an hour the blues band left the stage to enthusiastic applause, and Zeke and his mates appeared, arranging their equipment and checking sound levels. Then it was time for them to start their half-hour set in front of the judges, who were seated behind a huge table set up in the arena, facing the stage.

John could recall how, back in his school days, he had sneered at the songs sung by members of the Scripture Union group – he thought the lyrics were mostly boring and repetitive, although he liked some of the tunes. This time he decided that he would listen to the words as well as the music; he would see whether the songs had anything to say to him.

The first song was a fairly conventional gospel number, nothing special, although he was surprised at the skill of the lead guitar player and Zeke's singing was far better than he remembered from his Luboga College days. Then the band moved into a lively number, with a driving rhythm, and the words coming through the giant loud speakers complemented the insistence of the music:

Oh where can I find him?
Oh where can he be?
The one who'll share my sorrows,
The one who'll understand me,
The one who'll understand me.

Zeke was singing with assurance, stepping up the volume as he moved through the verses of the song.

I'm looking for a freedom-man,
Who'll bring me liberty.

Then the backing singers, in superb harmony, finished the verse with a response to the previous lines:

But he won for you your freedom
On a cross at Calvary,
On a cross at Calvary.

At the end of the song, the tempo was slowed right down, and Zeke's voice rang out unaccompanied:

> *I'm looking for a Lord in life,*
> *But is he far or near?*

And then the whole band in unison joined voices to sing:

> *My friends, his name is Jesus Christ*
> *And he is standing here,*
> *Yes, he is standing here.*

The audience applauded loudly, and John, joining in, said to himself, "Wow! They're much, much better than I thought. These guys are good." He wouldn't admit it to himself, but it wasn't just the music that was getting to him. Something about the lyrics — about finding freedom and understanding — was resonating with his deepest feelings, and he felt a shiver running up and down his spine.

The band ran through their repertoire with sustained enthusiasm. Again and again, John found the words of the songs touching his heart. One song seemed to have been written specially for him. Entitled 'No Way To Go', it was sung to a lilting ballad rhythm with an aching saxophone solo. John listened, as though mesmerised, to the hopeless yearning in Zeke's voice:

> *No way I see to the right, no way to the left.*
> *No way I see in front of me,*
> *And there's no turning back.*
> *Hopes and ambitions all are gone: crazy dreams*
> *   of youth.*
> *Happiness is all a lie: now I can see the truth.*

This was followed by an explosion of hope in the pounding rhythm of 'New Life in Jesus', as if in answer to the sadness of the previous song. John felt that the Gospel Bravos had taken their audience on a roller-coaster of word and music, never allowing them to remain in one mood or style.

Near the end of the half hour, Zeke addressed the audience. "Thank you for listening to us. We've really enjoyed playing for you! And now we've just got time for one last number. It's not one of our own songs. Many of you will remember Bobby K's big hit of a few years ago. Well, here's our own version... of 'The City Kid' rap."

As the band slipped easily into the rhythm of the song and Zeke Ochieng grasped the mike waiting for the conclusion of the intro, John's mind was transported back to his meeting with Zeke in Mkandu village after their final term at school. Once again those old familiar, half-mocking words rang out:

You think that with your modern clothes and the way
  you can dance,
With your mini-skirted girlfriends – that life's a game
  of chance.
You think that popularity will get you anywhere,
And when your pocket's full of money
Then you'll never have a care!

You think you'll get an office job in the swinging town.
You think you'll rise so quickly, your feet will soon leave
  the ground.
You think that men will whisper soft, what a splendid
  chap you are,

As you rocket past in the driving seat
Of your brand new Mercedes Benz car!

You think that fame and fortune will lead to paradise,
But the more you get, the more you want — it never
  satisfies.
You can gain the whole wide world, my friend, and lose
  your very soul;
And when you die what do you get?
A coffin and a small rectangular hole!

The audience was on its feet, applauding wildly, as Zeke and his band mates took a bow and ran off stage. John, however, was sitting with his head bowed, tears running down his cheeks. He felt that his life had been ripped open, and held up to public gaze.

ELEVEN

Convergent Paths

A few minutes later, John exited the stadium, determined to find Zeke before he disappeared from the scene. There were so many questions swirling around in his brain and he knew that Zeke would have some of the answers he needed. It had seemed that the Gospel Bravos had been performing their songs just for him – not to thrill or entertain, but to disturb and challenge. Yet surely they could not have known that he was sitting there in the audience?

Struggling along with the help of his crutch John scoured the car park behind the stadium. He could see a large white van with its rear doors still open. It looked uncomfortably familiar: that had to be the vehicle he had nearly crashed into. He thought he could recognise the figure of Zeke leaning against the side of the van. He called out but there was no reaction. He waved his crutch in the air – still no response. The figure turned his back and was about to enter the van.

Once again John shouted – this time at the top of his voice: "Zeke! Zeke Ochieng!" Now the figure turned and gazed in puzzlement in John's direction. It was obvious that he didn't recognise John from that distance, but he made his way towards the figure with the crutch and finally recognised his former school friend.

"What the. . . ? John? Is that you?"

"That's right, Zeke. It's me – again!"

"What happened?"

"Well, it wasn't me driving past a No Entry sign, if that's what you're thinking!"

The two young men shook hands and greeted each other. Once the greetings were over, John burst out: "Zeke, I've got to talk to you!"

"Of course – any time."

"No, Zeke, I need to talk to you now. It's important."

Zeke could hear the note of urgency in his friend's voice. "OK, John. I'll tell the others to leave without me." He hurried back to the van, spoke with the driver and waved as the vehicle drove off.

John watched the van weave its way through the packed cars towards the exit. Meanwhile, Zeke had returned to where John was standing, forlorn and motionless. "How are things, John?"

"Pretty bad, to be honest."

Zeke nodded. "OK, let's go to the café over there. We can have a chat over a soda."

They sat down at a table, ordered drinks and looked at each other questioningly.

"Well done on your performance, Zeke. Your band is really good."

"Thanks. But is that what you wanted to speak to me about?"

"Yes and no. It's a bit difficult to explain. You see..." John's voice trailed off, and the two sipped their drinks in silence. At last, Zeke asked, "How's your job at the Min-tech?"

"Not so good. I decided to – to leave..." Again, an awkward silence.

"Want to talk about it, John?"

"As a matter of fact, I would like to talk about it, if you've got time to listen?"

Zeke could hear the distress in the other's voice. "Of course I've got time. Go ahead."

"Well," John began hesitantly, "it's not easy. You see, I've made one mistake after another. The fact is, my life is in a complete mess. It began, I suppose, with a girl I knew called Rosemary..."

John told his story: Rosemary Kimaga. The Kirikiri nightclub. Expensive living and getting into debt. Mr Mwive and his corrupt smile. Promotion and Mr Molo's exit. The files he had doctored and the extra payments he had "earned". The threat of exposure by the Corruption Commission. Losing his girl to the Right Hon. Yakobo Njoru. His visit to Sikenyi and getting robbed and beaten up. Losing his car. Being dismissed from his job and evicted from his lodgings. His increasingly heavy drinking. Finally, John revealed, almost choking on his words, how he tried to take his own life by stepping in front of a speeding bus.

When John had started speaking, he had not intended to tell his friend so much of what had happened. But having

116

a willing listener, who seemed genuinely concerned, gave him the freedom to be open and honest. The lies and secrets that he had stored inside him were released, and John experienced, amidst his shame, a great wave of relief.

John continued, "When I left hospital earlier today, I felt completely empty. And aimless. No idea what to do with my life. Not even sure what my next move should be."

"You're worried about finding another job?"

"No, it's not that. Though I will need to get another job eventually, if I can."

"You're missing your girlfriend?"

"No – well, yes I do miss her in a way. But even if Rose came back to me now, I wouldn't be happy. I know it wouldn't work. Everything's changed. My old life is finished."

John's words were expressed in a tone that conveyed neither regret nor rejoicing. His old life was finished: this was the cold truth of certain knowledge. The more he thought about his life in the city, the less inclined he felt to mourn what he had lost. So much of his activity had been an act; even he and Rose had been playing out roles in front of each other, concealing more and more of their true selves as time went on.

The heat of the afternoon was still intense. Everywhere the ground was baked hard and dry. However, far away to the west grey clouds, with their promise of rain, were forming, John poked his crutch into the red earth near his table, stirring up dust.

"This has been a hell of a long dry season," he said.

"We can talk about the weather if you like, John," said Zeke, with gentle sarcasm.

117

John laughed. "No, that won't help! Let me tell you, Zeke – that song you used to sing – the one you ended your performance with..."

"You mean 'The City Kid'?"

"Yeah, that one. Those words. They're all so true. That song's about me, you know. I've been obsessed with all those things the song refers to – girls, money, popularity, putting on a good show and impressing others. And most people seem to be scrambling for the same things."

"So you got swept along with the current."

"That's right, Zeke. You get swept along. And nobody cares a damn whether you sink or swim. Like my colleagues in the office, when I got sacked."

"Like *you*, when the previous senior accounts clerk was pushed out of the way," added Zeke bluntly.

John nodded. "Yes, just like me. We've become carrion-eaters, feeding on other people's misfortunes."

"It's a big step to admit that."

"I suppose so, but I think I've known this deep-down for some time. For a long while I've been running away from facing up to the hard facts. But I'm not running any more." John placed his right hand on his wooden crutch. "Especially with this third leg."

Zeke smiled at his friend's joke. "You may not be running, John – but which direction are you facing?"

"I honestly don't know. But I saw the way you and your band played and sang those songs and I saw something – something real in your faces. When you sang that song 'Where Can I Find Him?', you know the one I mean?"

"Of course. I wrote the song."

118

"Well, when you sang about Jesus being the answer to all those deep needs – like the desire for freedom, for understanding and so on – those words got to me. Especially when you sang 'He is standing here'. And I wondered if it's really true? Or is it just the same fantasy that I rejected when we were at Luboga College."

Zeke restrained a flicker of anger and spoke quietly. "It was never a fantasy, John. But you've got to ask Christ into your life to experience the reality. It will always seem a bit of self-delusion from the outside."

"You really think your Jesus is the answer to my messed-up life?"

"He's not *my* Jesus. He's *everyone's* Jesus – everyone who wants to draw near to him and get to know him personally."

John shifted in his chair, staring vacantly towards the stadium, from where the sounds of a reggae group were drifting towards them. "Perhaps Jesus is alive and can live in people like you – decent, law-abiding folk who..."

"For goodness sake, John!" Zeke interrupted irritably. "I'm not an angel from heaven. You think I haven't done things I regret? Of course I have!"

"Yeah, but not like me. I've gone over the limit, like those drunk drivers."

"No you haven't. There isn't a limit to God's forgiveness. And anyway Jesus said that he had come to call sinners, not so-called righteous people, to repentance. Absolutely no one is too off-limit for Jesus' love and acceptance. You just have to believe that he died on the cross for you, then confess your sins and turn away from them."

John recalled their pointless arguments over religion while at school. "Now you're preaching at me, just like you used to!"

"Sorry. I didn't mean to. But be honest, John: God spoke to you in the stadium a short while ago. You know that, don't you?"

"It does seem that way, Zeke. It's like he's on my case. But I'm not sure about this idea of receiving Jesus into my life. Starting off in a completely new direction. It's all a bit scary, like a step into the unknown."

Zeke nodded. "I agree – it is a big step. But not entirely into the unknown. Many others have gone before you – like me, for example, like my band-mates. We have found God's love and grace. But it's not a step to take lightly. You need to weigh up some of the consequences."

"You're right, Zeke. I'm not interested in a fool's paradise."

"We need more time to talk," said Zeke, rising from his chair. "Where are you staying?"

John looked down, shame-faced. "I honestly don't know. I could go to my uncle's – but he'll pack me off to Mkandu at first light."

"That's OK. You can come back to college with me. I've got a room on campus and there's plenty of floor space."

"You sure, Zeke? I don't want to bother you."

"It's no bother. It'll be great to talk some more. Come on, let's go."

As the two young men left the café and made their way to the road, echoes of the distant booming of thunder from the west rumbled over their heads. John looked up at the cloudless sky. "About time we had some rain."

TWELVE

The Start of
Something New

Back at Kamobi Teachers' Training College, Zeke led John to his room in his hall of residence. It was on the second floor and John laboured to negotiate the stairs. There was no air-conditioning in the building, and the heat remained oppressive. The rumbling of thunder in the west had faded away and the air remained as dry as dust.

"You know, Zeke, I feel as dry as this city," John remarked. "Dry as a desert."

"It's only Jesus who can deal with that condition, John." Zeke took a Bible off his bookshelf and leafed through the pages of the New Testament. "Do you mind if I read you some verses?"

"Quote all you like, Zeke. I haven't looked at a Bible since we did R.E. at school."

Zeke quickly found the verse he was looking for. "Listen to what Jesus said to a woman who had messed up her life: *'Everyone who drinks of this water will be thirsty again.*

The water that I will give him will become in him a spring of water welling up to eternal life.'"

"And presumably Jesus wasn't talking about the liquid we now get from a tap! But it sounds too good to be true."

"No, but it's too true to be ignored. Jesus really can begin a new life in you. I'm not saying it will all be plain sailing. Becoming a Christian isn't like someone waving a magic wand and then suddenly all your problems vanish."

John nodded. "With all the problems I've got, that would be a fairy tale."

"Yes, well, it's not a fairy tale, but no one can decide for you. It's your decision."

John held his hands up in a gesture of uncertainty. "Zeke, I'd like to open my life to Christ. But I don't know how to pray. Can you pray for me?"

The two young men bowed their heads and Zeke prayed a simple prayer of repentance, faith and trust – claiming the promise of Jesus: *"If anyone hears my voice and opens the door, I will come in to him and eat with him, and he with me."*

At the end of the prayer, John said "Amen", and, once again, as he had done at the stadium, he found his eyes watering and tears were running down his cheeks. At first he tried to resist, but the dam was broken: great sobs shook his body.

He was weeping for the wasted months and years; for the way he had lied, cheated and deceived; for the way that greed and selfish desire had directed his life; the way he had for so long closed his mind to the Good News of Christ, thinking he was far too "cool" to get sucked into religion;

was weeping for the way he had tried to kill himself
nearly succeeded.

But he was also weeping for joy, for God had given him
another chance in life. He was like Lazarus, the man in the
Bible whom Jesus awoke from the tomb of death: it seemed
to John that he too had come back from the dead.

The two friends carried on talking into the night, but
both were tired from the day's activities so they agreed to
get some sleep. Zeke insisted that John should use his bed,
while he lay on a blanket on the floor. It was still very hot
in the room, but exhaustion eventually brought sleep. As he
drifted into slumber, John could hear the renewed booming
of thunder far off, but now getting closer; and the night
sky was illuminated from time to time by the reflections of
lightning strikes below the western horizon.

* * * * *

John was stripped to the waist and dripping with sweat
as he slammed the heavy pickaxe into the rich seam. He
could see diamond-bearing rock in front of him, and a mad
compulsion was urging him to break into the seam, even
though he could hear the crash of rocks that were falling
from above. There was a sudden explosion of sound from
the rim of the open-cast mine. He looked up. Another huge
detonation followed and he saw a long vertical split opening
up in the wall of the mine above him. A moment later an
avalanche of rocks and earth surged down the steep slope
towards him. In an instant he was enveloped in a thunderous
wall of debris and he cried out for help, "Oh God, please help

me!" He was choking to death but, just when all hope was gone, he felt himself being gently lifted up from the chaos at the bottom of the mine towards the light above him — lifted clear of the upward-facing mouth of the mine and laid softly on a grassy bank by a wide river, whose steady, reassuring throb replaced the fearful thunder of the mine. The water was spilling over the banks of the river and bathing his body in cool water. John was aware of the presence of someone sitting by his prostrate body, speaking words of assurance. He couldn't identify the voice but he felt totally secure. And then John slipped into a dreamless sleep.

* * * * *

Outside the room where John slept, the great storm announcing the start of the rainy season had spent its first fury over the city, lighting up the sky with flashes and pounding the air with thunder. Now the storm was over and the only sound was the constant, hypnotic, reassuring roar of tropical rain.

John woke at first light. The dream about the diamond mine was still sharply etched in his imagination. And he could still sense the presence of the One — surely that was Jesus? — who had lifted him from disaster and laid him by the flowing river.

Zeke was still fast asleep, curled up on his blanket on the floor. Anxious not to disturb him, John stepped carefully over him and stood by the window, which he opened wide.

The rain had ceased but the air was clear and sweet. The land had been cleansed of dust and dryness by the night's storm, and the moist greens of trees, grass and new shoots stood out freshly against the red earth.

New life was beginning all over the city, it seemed. The season of unremitting heat was past. John felt strangely at one with the earth; for he too had been washed clean and was on the brink of a new life.

"Thank you for saving me," he prayed silently to the God he was just getting to know.

For a few more days, he stayed with Zeke, learning to read the Bible and discovering the wonder of prayer. However, although there was a lot of happiness in John's new life, a dark cloud still hung over him.

Among the people he had hurt, the ones who had perhaps suffered most were his family, especially his mother. He had not visited home since his dad's funeral the previous year and he hadn't phoned home for months. In asserting his independence, he had left his mother out of his life; she had practically ceased to exist for John in his mad, frenetic life in the city. But now John's conscience cried out at the cruelty of his behaviour. He had repaid the love of his parents and family with indifference.

"I must go home to Mkandu and see my family," John told Zeke as they were having breakfast together one morning in college. "You remember Mkandu? That forgotten corner of the country which I used to mock so much? Well, I don't feel in the mood for mocking now. I've treated them very badly. Specially my mother. She and dad sweated their guts out to pay for my school fees – and I just took it for granted. I need to go home and come clean about my mistakes – and ask forgiveness."

126

Zeke replied, "I'm sure you're right, John. You can stay here as long as you like — but when you're ready for that journey, just say so. And I'll make sure you get on the right bus!"

John's impatience to be on his way grew as the week passed. His thoughts kept returning to his home village and to the extended family living there and in the surrounding area. He wondered how his mother would react when he arrived, penniless, jobless and physically battered. However difficult that meeting might prove, it was something which had to be done. He would be bringing a lot of bad news with him, but he hoped that his family would be able to share in the good news that he had begun a new life.

A couple of days later, John and Zeke were weaving their way through the maze of parked buses at the central bus station. The scene seemed like chaos, but actually all the drivers knew exactly where to park their bus and how to negotiate their tortuous way between all the other vehicles to the exit. John felt particularly nervous moving among the buses. He knew what they were capable of.

They found the sign that indicated the bus route that went east of the capital, passing close to Mkandu village. A few people were waiting but the bus had not yet arrived. They sat down on a rough bench and waited.

John turned to Zeke. "I want to thank you for everything you've done for me. You've been more than a friend. We must keep in contact."

"Sure. You've got my number. And I'll see you when you come back to the hospital to get that plaster off your leg."

An old, battered bus edged its way towards them, its

engine straining with the effort. In front it bore the legend: *Trust in the Lord*.

Zeke helped John climb the steps into the bus and then handed up his crutch. They shook hands vigorously. John took a seat by a window at the front and waved to his friend as the bus, nearly fully loaded with passengers, moved away. Zeke gave him a thumbs-up sign and watched the bus disappear from sight.

Soon the bus was roaring down Aggrey Avenue, past the spot where John had nearly thrown his life away. Fifteen minutes later it had escaped the worst of the traffic in the city centre and was climbing the hill out of the city. John looked back at the diminishing skyline of offices, banks, hotels and government ministries. They did not seem as proud or imposing as when he had first seen them. He wondered whether he would ever return to live or work there, in the heart of the city. He did not know. But he did know – with the certainty of a man reborn – that he would never again act the part of the city kid.

Discussion Questions

1. John Ouma is an ambitious young man. Do you think there is there anything wrong with being ambitious? How important do you think integrity is when you're trying to get on in life? Do you think the means sometimes justifies the end?

2. What do you think of Zeke Ochieng? Do you think he is he too outspoken about his religious views?

3. Do you think Rose and John made a good couple? What/who do you blame for the breakdown in their relationship?

4. John falls prey to greed and corruption. How likely is it that you will face similar pressures in your life? What other potential pitfalls in life start off small, but can spiral out of control? How could you avoid anything like that happening to you?

5. John Ouma's reaction to losing everything that seemed to give meaning to his life was to attempt to take his own life. Was this a logical or rational reaction? If you had a friend thinking about ending their life, how could you help them?

6. John's encounter with Zeke at the music festival was a life-saver for him. Would you regard this as good fortune or do you think that God might work through coincidences like this?

7. What do you think about the idea of finding a "message in the music"? Are song and music important and can they really change lives? If so, how does that work? Could you name a piece of music that means something to you?

8. Zeke extends the hand of genuine, practical help to John after they meet at the music festival. Do you know someone going through a hard time who could really use your help?

9. What does this story imply about the importance of being a Christian? Is this something you agree with, or not?

10. If you were John's friend, what advice would you give him as he boards the bus to return home?

If you enjoyed this story, check out other books for young people at: www.dernierpublishing.com

What is a Christian?

If you have read this book, and wondered what it means to be a Christian, here's a quick explanation:

First we need to go back to the beginning. Christians believe that God made the heavens and the earth, and everything in it. At first everything was perfect, but sadly, people deliberately disobeyed God, and "sin" came into the world. That's bad things like lying, stealing and cheating. We have all done these things, and had these things done to us. We know what it's like.

Our sin separates us from God (who is perfect in every way), so we needed someone to take the punishment in our place. Justice has to be done. Sin has to be paid for.

Because he loved us so much and wanted to make a way for us to live with him again, God the Father sent his Son, Jesus, into the world. Jesus was born in Bethlehem at the time of the Romans, and lived a perfect life. Jesus took on himself the punishment we deserved for our sin, when he died on a cross – he hadn't sinned like we do, but he died in our place. (It's a bit like someone paying someone else's debt.)

Three days later, Jesus rose from the dead – he defeated death!

We don't deserve God's forgiveness, but if we are truly sorry for our sin and decide to walk in his ways instead of ours, he not only promises to forgive us, but gives us his Holy Spirit to live with us forever. So when we are a Christian, we will go on living with God in heaven after our bodies die. This means we have eternal life!

So a Christian is someone who:

1. Has turned to God

2. Has had their sins forgiven

3. Follows Jesus (that means following his example)

4. Has the Holy Spirit living in them

5. Is looking forward to heaven!

We know all this though the Bible, which is God's word – it's a great book. :-)

Would you like to be a Christian?

If you would like to become a Christian you need to take the following steps:

1. Be sure it's what you want to do. Think carefully. Are you truly sorry for your sin? Do you really want to follow Jesus?

2. If you do, you need to pray. That means talk to God. You can do it anywhere, any time. (Not only did he make the whole world and everything in it, but God knows everything about us and hears us when we pray. Awesome!)

3. Here's a first prayer you can use if you like. (It starts Dear Lord – many prayers say "Lord" when they are talking about God, because when you are a Christian, Jesus becomes the Lord of your life, which means you

do what he wants, not what you want... you will find out more about this as you grow as a Christian.)

Dear Lord, I'm truly sorry for my sin. I realise now that my sin has stopped me from knowing you in the past, but I believe you died in my place. I'd like to follow you from now on. Please forgive me and send me your Holy Spirit, so I will be with you forever. Amen.

(Amen is a word often used at the end of a prayer. It means "let it be so".)

4. Now you need to get to know God! Here are some steps you need to take:

First, tell someone you have prayed. Who will you tell? Do it right now! You can contact us, too – we would love to hear from you. Read the Bible. Find the book of Matthew (it's the first book of the New Testament), get yourself a bookmark, and start reading! Read a bit every day. You can read the Bible online if you haven't got a Bible yourself.

Carry on praying. You can pray all the time, any time, anywhere – it is the most wonderful, amazing thing to talk to God who made the whole world and everything in it! You might like to just talk about how you feel. You might like to thank him for the good things in your life. You might like to ask him to help you with things you find difficult. It's fine to make up your own prayer – you can just talk, as if you were talking to a close friend or a loving father, because from now on

Jesus will be your friend and God will be your Father in heaven! Or you can find some prayers online or in a book if you like. You can pray out loud or in your head because God even knows the thoughts of our hearts.

Go to church with a friend or your family. Everyone who is a Christian needs to spend time with other Christians. If you don't know any other Christians, pray the Lord will help you find some, especially if you live in a country where there aren't many Christians and churches.

Remember this:
God loves you more than you can imagine!

He knows everything about you, even your thoughts.

He will always be with you – he will never abandon you or leave you alone.

If God's Holy Spirit lives in you, you have been "born again" in your spirit.

If you have asked for forgiveness and are truly sorry, you will be forgiven – it's a promise!

Because we are human, we will keep on getting it wrong, but every time we ask for forgiveness, we will be washed clean once again.

However you feel, trust in God. You know how on a cloudy day you can't see the sun? It's still there, though! In the same way, you might not always feel that God is with you, but he is there just the same.

If you have any questions, or would you like to contact any of our authors, please do so through the contact form on the Dernier Publishing website:

www.dernierpublishing.com
We look forward to hearing from you!